*Violet realized that the room had grown quiet as
everyone stopped talking. She could feel
that all eyes were on her.*

The king cleared his throat. "So, we have you
to thank for the safe return of our son?" he
asked.

Violet glanced at Richard, who was nodding
his head. She hadn't been the only one to care for
the prince. Her parents and Father Paul had aided
him as well. Still, from the look in Richard's eyes
she could tell this was no time for her to be humble.
"Yes," Violet said.

"My dear, we owe a debt of gratitude to your
family for caring for our son while he was ill. We
would like to reward you. However, only a princess
can enter the competition," the king said, his voice
still gentle.

"And a princess stands before you," Violet said,
raising her chin.

"Once upon a Time"
is Timeless with these Retold Tales:

ONCE UPON A TIME

Violet Eyes

DEBBIE VIGUIÉ

SIMON PULSE
New York   London   Toronto   Sydney

This book is a work of fiction. Any references to historical events, real people,
or real locales are used fictitiously. Other names, characters, places, and incidents
are the product of the author's imagination, and any resemblance to actual
events or locales or persons, living or dead, is entirely coincidental.

SIMON PULSE
An imprint of Simon & Schuster Children's Publishing Division
1230 Avenue of the Americas, New York, NY 10020
First Simon Pulse paperback edition February 2010
Copyright © 2010 by Debbie Viguié
All rights reserved, including the right of
reproduction in whole or in part in any form.
SIMON PULSE and colophon are registered trademarks
of Simon & Schuster, Inc.
For information about special discounts for bulk purchases,
please contact Simon & Schuster Special Sales at 1-866-506-1949 or
business@simonandschuster.com.
The Simon & Schuster Speakers Bureau can bring authors to your live
event. For more information or to book an event contact the Simon & Schuster
Speakers Bureau at 1-866-248-3049 or visit our website at
www.simonspeakers.com.
The text of this book was set in Adobe Jenson.
Manufactured in the United States of America
2 4 6 8 10 9 7 5 3 1
Library of Congress Control Number 2009928029
ISBN 978-1-4169-8676-8
ISBN 978-1-4391-5744-2 (eBook)

To all those who still believe in fairy tales

ACKNOWLEDGMENTS

I would like to thank my fantastic editor, Annette Pollert, for all her enthusiasm and support. I would also like to thank Beth Jusino for being a great agent. As usual, I couldn't have written this book without the love and support of my friends and family. Thank you all very much.

CHAPTER ONE

A storm was coming. The air seemed heavy and charged, and the wind had begun blowing from the east with a singular intensity of purpose. It brought with it the smell of distant rain. Violet stood in the middle of her father's wheat field, closed her eyes, and threw out her arms as if to embrace the storm.

Every great or terrible moment of her life had been presaged by a storm, and Violet had learned to accept and embrace change as part of life. To meet it, not fear it. It had stormed the night before her brother was born, and four years later it stormed the night before he died. It had stormed the day before her cousin Tara's wedding, where Violet had kissed a boy for the first time. It had stormed just before the beginning of the two-year drought that had nearly destroyed her family's farm. And when a storm had come to save them from starvation, she had danced in it.

She took a deep breath, feeling the storm as it moved in. It was as though the tempest called to something deep and wild within her. She opened her eyes, and she could see the rain approaching. Violet watched as it hit the tops of the trees in the forest and came on with a steady sweep.

"Child, come inside before the storm arrives," her father, William, said, approaching from the barn, where he had just put away Bessie and the wagon. It was the first Monday of the month, and he had just returned from his monthly trip into the village. Violet was bursting to ask him what news he had heard, but she knew better. Her father always saved news for telling at the supper table. She gave him a little wave, wanting to linger a few more moments and knowing that she would hear the news soon enough.

She turned aside reluctantly as her father came to stand beside her. He looked out at the rain sweeping in, and a worried look crossed his weather-beaten face. "I hope that storm doesn't damage the crops," he said.

Violet smiled. He was always so practical.

"But isn't there something beautiful about it, Father?"

"Yes, so long as it doesn't destroy anything." He turned and headed for the house, clearly expecting her to follow.

Violet lingered another moment and cast one last look at the storm front. "But it always does," she muttered under her breath before turning and heading after her father.

Just outside of the barn they were met by Thomas, the butcher's son. Thomas was thirteen and fast growing into a man. He was the youngest of six children, all boys. For the last four years Thomas had worked for Violet's father. As the farm prospered and William grew older, he had needed more help. With no son and only one daughter William had had to look elsewhere. Thomas was a good lad and worked hard for the few coins William could pay him and the chance to learn a trade other than his father's. The village was small and would never have need of so many butchers.

William tousled the boy's hair fondly. "You did well today, lad. You staying for supper?"

Thomas shook his head. "I'd like to get home before the storm hits."

"There's a wise lad. Off with you, then, and we'll see you in the morning less'n the storm hasn't let up. If it's still raining, don't bother coming until the day after."

Thomas nodded his understanding before taking off toward home at a long, loping run.

"He should just make it before the rain starts," her father said, as much to himself as to Violet.

Inside the house the smell of stew filled the air. Violet's mother, Sarah, was already ladling the broth and bits of vegetables out into bowls on the table. Finished, she put down the pot and coughed hard into her apron.

"Storm's coming," her father said. "If there's anything you need from outside, Mother, one of us'll fetch it. We wouldn't want you to catch cold. You'll want to bundle up warm tonight."

"I'm fine, really," her mother answered with a weak smile.

Violet wasn't so sure that was true. For the last three months her mother had been coughing, not hard, but persistently. She knew Father was worried, even though he didn't say much. No one wanted to talk about the fact that Mother was getting weaker.

Father was usually cheerful and talked a lot during supper. Usually, on the days he went to the village, he was bursting with news, but this time he sat silently. It soon became obvious as they ate, though, that there was something on his mind. He ate in a distracted manner, casting occasional glances outside that grew more frequent once the rain began to fall.

"What's wrong, William?" Sarah asked at last.

Violet's father looked up and gave his wife a weak smile. "I'm just hoping the crops weather the storm."

Sarah looked puzzled. "Why is this storm more troubling to you than others?" she asked.

He sighed and put down the piece of bread he had been eating. "The steward sent word from the castle that they're going to need twice as much wheat and vegetables for this year's Feasting than last."

Violet stared at her father, wide-eyed, as her mother gasped. "Twice! Are they planning to feed the whole kingdom?"

The Feasting was four weeks away. It was an annual event which commemorated the victory of the people of Cambria over the king of Lore in their last great war. The Feasting would last for four days, the height of which was the High Feast on the third day, when no one in Cambria did any work. Rumor had it that during the High Feast the servants in the castle even ate with the lords. For the common people High Feast Day was a day of revelry and a festival. Everyone would sample strange foreign foods, dance, and make music while engaging in contests of skill and strength. Next to Christmas it was Violet's favorite day of the year.

"More like they'll be feeding royalty from other kingdoms," her father answered her mother. "They say it'll be a very special celebration this year. They say the Prince will marry."

Violet sat up straighter, eager to hear. Any wedding was special, but a royal wedding! There had not been one in her lifetime. "Who is he to marry?" she asked.

William shook his head. "No one knows. It seems it's something of a mystery. But they say royal carriages have been arriving at the castle for the last fortnight."

"But they don't know who the bride will be?" Sarah asked.

William shook his head. "Some say she was in one of those carriages; others say she hasn't arrived yet. One thing that is certain is that no one really knows. I did talk to one of the kitchen boys who works in the castle. He told me that the reason nobody knows who the prince will marry is that the prince doesn't know himself."

"How can the prince not know?" Violet asked, bewildered.

"The lad said that princesses had been arriving from all over and that there was some sort of contest to be held."

A contest! The thought seemed outrageous, and yet at the same time it appealed to Violet. Cambria was one of the strongest kingdoms, and it made sense that all of the other kingdoms would prize an alliance such as marriage could bring.

"Well, I never," Sarah said, shaking her head. "That reminds me, though. Violet, are you still planning to enter one of the contests at the festival this year?"

"I was planning to," Violet said, turning toward her mother. "I was thinking maybe the maze."

"You've a good sense of direction; you'd stand a fair chance," her mother said.

"You could try and ride Bessie in the girls' riding contest," her father added. "You're a fair hand with her."

"You could bake one of your berry pies," her mother suggested.

"I've been thinking of those three," Violet admitted. "I'm just not sure which to enter."

"There's nothing to stop you from entering all three of them," William said. "And wouldn't that be a sight if you won them all?" He leaned back in his chair with a grin.

"You're putting an awful lot of store in my skills," Violet said, laughing.

They laughed some more about the festival, but they were all tired, so after cleaning up the dinner dishes they headed to bed. Violet drew the curtain she and her mother had hung so she could have some privacy and curled up on her bed to listen to the storm outside. The wind was howling fiercely, as if looking for a way inside the house. She pulled her blanket up under her chin and listened to the sound of the rain as it hit the roof. Violet thought about the conversation at dinner. She couldn't help but wonder about the prince and the woman he was to marry.

Prince Richard could see the storm clouds gathering and debated what to do. He was less than a day's journey from home, but it seemed prudent to stop for the night and wait out the storm. If his memory served him, there was a small farming village about an hour's ride away. They might have an inn. If not, Richard was sure any of his subjects would volunteer their homes for him.

"What do you say, Baron? Rest tonight and ride home after the storm?" Prince Richard asked, stroking his stallion's gray neck. The horse nickered as if in agreement. "You're right. We've been gone nearly a year; another day more or less won't matter."

He pointed Baron's nose toward the village before giving the horse his head. They trotted along at a slow, comfortable pace for both animal and rider. The truth was, as much as he missed home, Prince Richard was not eager to return.

For as long as he could remember, his parents had been taken with the idea of him marrying a "true" princess. In their minds this was a princess of refinement and breeding and the utmost sensitivity. When Prince Richard had turned seventeen, they had sent him out into the world to meet as many princesses as he could. Despite the king and queen's years of lecturing, they still didn't seem to trust Richard to find his own bride. So Prince Richard had had to invite each of the princesses to visit his home in the weeks before the annual Feasting, where his parents would meet her and judge her worth.

The entire thing was appalling to him. Prince Richard had felt overwhelmed with embarrassment at the first castle, wondering how he could tell the king and queen that their daughter would be evaluated by his parents before she could be eligible to marry him. What Richard had discovered, though, had upset and embarrassed him even more. Prince Richard had found that the women he met practically fell over themselves at the opportunity to prove their worth to his parents. Their parents had also seemed to approve of the whole process. Prince Richard didn't know if the excitement had been generated by a deep sense of respect for his parents or because the lives of these people were so structured and confining that they found the challenge appealing.

"How many princesses have we met, Baron, eh?" Richard asked the stallion, who shook his head as if to say the number was too high to count.

"At least forty. I wonder how many of them are already waiting for us at the castle." He sighed. The prospect was disturbing. Richard believed with all his heart that the man should prove himself worthy, not the woman.

The first raindrops began to fall, sooner than he had anticipated. After a moment's hesitation Richard turned Baron from the road and into a field. He could see smoke rising in the distance and reasoned that cross-country would be the fastest way to the village. He touched his heels to Baron's flanks, and the great horse sprang forward into a gallop. Richard leaned forward, enjoying the feel of the wind on his face.

They had been galloping for no more than a minute when the skies opened up and the rain began to lash them. The cold of it seeped into Prince Richard's bones, and he found himself shivering and urging Baron on faster. The horse plunged down into a small ravine, splashed across a swiftly rising river, and then charged up the other side.

They had just made it back to level land when something went wrong. Richard felt an unsettling sensation of sliding sideways as Baron slipped in the mud. The horse staggered, regained his footing, but then two strides later fell without warning. Richard, still unseated, flew over his horse's head and landed on the ground. His head struck something hard, and he felt a flash of stabbing pain before everything went black.

☙ ☙ ☙

The storm subsided some time after midnight. Lying awake, Violet listened to the rain as it gradually passed, and she couldn't help but wonder what change it would bring to her life. She thought about the upcoming royal wedding, drifting to dreams of her own wedding.

At seventeen Violet was old enough to marry, and many of her friends and neighbors already had. Still, her parents hadn't spoken of choosing a husband for her. Violet herself had brought up the subject a year earlier, only to be told by her father that she was too young to think of such things and not to worry. She had tried to do as he said, but Violet found she couldn't put the thought completely from her mind. Every time she was in the village and her eyes would meet those of a young man, she would wonder to herself if he was the one.

It wasn't that Violet was eager to marry, but neither was she afraid of it, as many girls of her acquaintance were. Rather, Violet had been increasingly aware of a kind of restlessness, a sense of not belonging as she had gotten older. The only way she could explain it was as having made the transformation from child to woman and feeling the pressing awareness that someday soon she must be the mistress of her own household and not the child in her parents'.

And so, as the last of the rain ceased, Violet fell asleep with an eager sense of anticipation for the change that she felt sure was coming.

CHAPTER TWO

Violet and her parents were up with the dawn. The three were finishing breakfast when they heard Thomas shouting outside.

In two strides William was at the door, yanking it open. "What's the matter?" he asked tersely.

Past her father Violet could see Thomas, his hair disheveled and his eyes wide. "There's a man in the field. His horse threw him, and he's hurt."

It took only a moment for William to pull on his boots. "Mother, better prepare a place for this stranger. Violet, come with us. We might need you to hold the horse."

Violet jumped up from the table, grabbing an apple as she did so.

Outside the house Violet could see a horse standing a ways off, his head bent toward something on the ground she couldn't quite see. William and Thomas both trotted toward the horse, and Violet had to run to keep up. When they drew close, she saw a man crumpled on the ground.

The horse touched the man with his nose before turning toward them and stamping his feet angrily. His ears were swept back along his head, and his eyes glared wickedly. Violet sucked in her breath. The horse was magnificent. She had never seen his like. His dark gray skin was stretched over massive muscles. His mane and tail were black as night. He was no common plow horse, nor the kind of riding horse owned by a messenger, nor a cart horse owned by anyone in the village.

Her eyes traveled from the horse to his master, who lay on the ground, his rich clothes covered with mud. A shock of black hair as dark as the horse's mane topped a pale face. What looked like dried blood matted part of the hair and had been smeared across his cheek.

Thomas took a step forward, and the horse became more agitated and screamed what seemed a warning. The horse reared and came back down with such force that the ground shook.

"Careful—if we upset the horse, he might trample his master," William said.

"Then what are we going to do?" Thomas asked.

"Let me try," Violet said. She turned and walked several paces away from Thomas and her father. She turned back and saw the horse staring at her, one ear flicking forward curiously. Violet stared back at the horse and then slowly extended her hand, holding the apple she had taken from the table.

Now both ears pricked forward, and the great beast regarded Violet with intense interest. He shifted his weight from one front hoof to the other as though trying to make a decision. Then, slowly, the horse moved away from his master and began to walk toward her, his desire for the apple outweighing his suspicion.

"You want this apple, Sir Horse?" she asked. The horse's bearing was so regal Violet fought the urge to curtsy to him. It seemed absurd, but it was as though the horse knew he was her better and was deigning to acknowledge her presence only because of the apple.

"Well then, good sir, you will have to show fine manners," she said.

The horse paused a couple of steps from Violet, but she did not move. Finally, he came forward and took the apple out of her hand. After he had crunched it down, he nuzzled her, clearly looking for more.

"I don't have any more, but I can get you some apples if you come with me," Violet said. She placed her hand on his nose, and he allowed the contact, stepping forward to lip at her skirts.

Violet slid her hand under his muzzle and gathered the reins loosely in her hand. Then she slid her other hand onto his neck and slowly began to pull the reins over his head so that they hung down from his mouth. Finally, Violet took a firmer hold on the end of the reins. Now she could lead him to the barn.

Violet glanced past the horse and saw that her father and Thomas were lifting the injured man between them. She stroked the horse's nose and then took a step toward the barn. The horse stood still for a moment before rearing up. Violet let the reins slide through her hands, but she didn't let go. His hooves crashed back down to the ground.

"Are you done showing off?" she asked, giving a slight tug on the reins. The horse stood stubbornly for a minute before taking a reluctant step forward, then another.

Violet turned to face the barn, and he followed. Behind her she could hear her father and Thomas talking.

"I ain't never seen a traveler dressed as him," Thomas said. "Who do you reckon he is?"

"A nobleman on his way to the castle, or a church-man, maybe."

A nobleman, definitely, Violet thought, glancing again at the horse. As they neared the barn, the stallion picked up his pace and began to nicker. From inside the barn Bessie, their mare, answered. The stallion jumped forward, nearly yanking Violet's arm from its socket. He plunged into the barn toward the stall where Bessie stood stretching her head out toward him. The horse's shoulder struck Violet, nearly knocking her over. She realized that within moments she would lose all control over him.

With all her strength Violet yanked hard on the reins. The stallion paused, startled, and turned to look at her. She pulled hard, and he followed her into the stall next to Bessie's. Violet turned him around, and then he began to kick. His mighty hooves crashed into the wall of the barn with a resounding thud. Violet hooked a finger into the buckle securing his bridle. Releasing it, she stepped out of the stall in one swift motion. The bridle slid off, and Violet closed the door just as he lunged toward her. The horse kicked the closed door, and Violet took a shaky breath.

"When you've calmed yourself, maybe we can get that saddle off," she told him while carefully hanging up his bridle. "I'll come back later and bring more apples like I promised."

Violet closed the barn door on her way out but could still hear the horse's persistent whinnies. She only hoped his master wouldn't be as much trouble once he was awake.

Thinking of the man she had seen, Violet's heart caught in her throat. She wasn't sure why, but she felt that his appearance on the heels of the storm was not a coincidence. Violet walked toward the house, her steps sure but her heart fluttering beneath her breast.

Inside the house there was a flurry of activity. Violet entered and then pressed her back to the door to keep out of the way as she took in the scene.

The man was lying on her bed. He was dressed in a warm, clean shirt and pair of pants that she recognized as belonging to her father. The man's sodden, filthy clothes lay in a pile in the corner.

Violet's mother had set to work washing the wound on the man's head, and he groaned but didn't wake up. She glanced up and, seeing Violet, motioned her over.

"Here, wash away the blood and dirt as best you can. I'll see what I can do with his clothes. Once he's clean, bundle him up so he doesn't catch a chill. Poor man was probably lying out there all night. I'm heating stew that he can eat when he wakes."

"Where'd you put the horse, lass?" William asked.

"In the stall next to Bessie. I got his bridle off, but he was too wild for me to try and take off his saddle. I figured maybe he would calm down and I could try again in a couple of hours," she said. Her father nodded approval.

Violet seated herself on her bed next to the stranger, taking the damp cloth and the washbasin from her mother. She applied the cloth to his forehead and marveled as she got a closer look at him. The man had a strong face with a broad brow, straight nose, and chiseled jaw. She memorized the lines of his face as she bathed it.

It took a while to loosen the blood and dirt from his hair, but eventually she finished. Violet was relieved to see that the cut, while long, was not deep. She bade her father come look at it. William examined the wound for a minute before straightening with a satisfied look on his face.

"He should come through just fine," William said, "long as he doesn't get the chill. Bundle him up."

Violet did as she was told and wrapped several thick warm blankets around the man, tucking them in around his feet. As she finished, the man began to mutter. She leaned close but could only make out one word he was saying over and over. She stood slowly, puzzled and wondering why the word "sensitive" was so important to him.

At last there was nothing left to do but wait until the stranger awoke. William went outside to tend the fields. And armed with three apples Violet headed to the barn.

Violet was relieved to discover that the stallion had calmed himself considerably. He even looked glad to see her, although she was sure that had more to do with the apples she was carrying than with her. Violet set two of them down outside the stall and held the third out to him as a peace offering. He took it from her and munched happily as Violet slipped into the stall.

The horse stood still and let her take off his saddle. After she had put it away, she returned to his stall with a brush. He flicked his tail contentedly as she brushed out his coat. She also cleaned the packed dirt out of his hooves. The stallion seemed to be in good shape, so whatever accident had befallen his rider had left him unaffected. Finished, Violet offered the horse the second apple. A small whinny from Bessie led Violet to rub the mare's nose and give her the third apple, a rare treat that the mare relished.

"Well, good sir and lady, that's the last of the apples for the day," Violet told them. She forked some hay into a feeding trough for each of them. When she was satisfied that the visitor had been made as comfortable as possible, Violet headed back to the house.

"How's he doing?" Violet asked her mother, who was busy cleaning the kitchen.

"Better. I think he's going to wake soon," her mother said. "Go keep an eye on him."

Dutifully, Violet pulled a chair up next to her bed and watched the stranger. He was stirring, and after a minute his eyelids fluttered open to reveal beautiful dark green eyes.

Prince Richard groaned as he began to wake up to find that his head was pounding fiercely. He was dimly aware of being indoors and of lying on something that was only marginally softer than the ground he had landed on. He forced his eyes open and blinked rapidly, trying to focus his vision. When everything grew clear, he saw the anxious face of a girl sitting near him.

She was very beautiful, in a wild sort of way. Her skin was deeply tanned, indicating that she spent a lot of time outdoors. Long honey-colored hair cascaded over her shoulders. Her smile was genuine, and it lit up her face. Most amazing, though, were her eyes. They were a strange, pale shade of purple, and they stared at him with as much curiosity as he was feeling about her. As Richard stared back at the girl, her lovely eyes seemed to widen.

"Is it you?" she whispered, so low he almost didn't hear her.

Richard blinked, not sure what she meant. "Who are you?" he asked, for the moment more interested in that than in knowing where he was.

"Violet," she answered simply. "And you are?"

The question took him somewhat by surprise. "Richard, of course," he said.

A glimmer of recognition flickered in her eyes, but before either of them could say anything more, a man appeared, a farmer by his look.

"Well, here you are, awake," the man boomed in a deep voice.

"So it would seem," Richard answered. "Although I'm not altogether sure where 'here' is."

The man laughed a deep rumble that seemed to shake the room. "You're in my home, and welcome. I'm William. We found you and your horse out in my field. This here is my daughter, Violet. My wife, Sarah, is fetching you some hot soup."

If he had been another man, Richard might have corrected William. William was a farmer, but the fields he tended did not belong to him. They belonged to the king, as did all the other land in the kingdom. But there was something so earnest and good-natured about William that Richard let it go. The man meant no offense and clearly took his job seriously. Instead Richard asked, "How's Baron?"

"Who?" William asked, looking puzzled.

"My horse. Is he hurt?"

"He's fine," the girl, Violet, assured him. "He was very upset at first, but he has calmed down and is eating now."

"That's a relief. Thank you for looking after him."

"It was no trouble, really," Violet said.

"So, traveler, where do you hail from?" William asked.

Richard smiled. "From here, from Cambria. I have been on a long journey, and I am on my way home. I was heading for the village to look for lodging when my horse fell in a patch of mud. I think I struck my head on something."

Richard wasn't sure why he wanted to put off telling them he was the prince. He supposed that it was because it was strange and somewhat pleasurable to have this simple man talk to him so honestly, so bluntly, as one man to another and not as a subject to his sovereign.

"You did. There was a stone next to you when we found you. I've sent to town for Father Paul. He's a priest, but he knows a fair bit about doctoring animals and people, too. He should be here soon."

"You didn't have to go to that trouble."

"'Twere no trouble. I reckon you're going to be fine, but it doesn't hurt to have him take a look. It wouldn't do to let a nobleman die in my house, would it?"

And there it was. The subtle question about who Richard was, though William realized that it was not his place to demand such an answer from a man of higher rank. Richard mustered a smile. "No, it wouldn't. And if that nobleman happened to be Prince Richard, it would be especially troublesome."

William gasped, and there was the sound of breaking pottery as Sarah dropped the bowl of stew she was carrying. The girl, Violet, just sat quietly, having already guessed that he was *that* Richard.

"Forgive me, Your Highness," William said when he found his voice. "I meant no disrespect by speaking with you so familiar." He dropped clumsily to his knees and bowed.

Richard put out his hand and touched William's shoulder. "Arise, honorable William. You have done me no discourtesy. It is I who should apologize to you for not having made myself known sooner. And I'm afraid I gave your good lady a fright. I shall be happy to pay for the broken bowl and for the inconvenience I have brought upon you all."

"No, what is ours is yours," William said, rising back to his feet. Violet rose to take a fresh bowl of stew from her mother and hand it to Richard. Then she went to sweep up the broken bits of pottery while Sarah mopped up the spilled soup.

The broth was hot, and it felt good sliding down Richard's throat. There was a bit of salt pork in it along with leeks, spinach, and cabbage. He also tasted some garlic. Altogether it was not very appetizing, but the emptiness in his stomach urged him to eat. "This is fine stew, milady, and thank you," he said to Sarah.

She blushed furiously and returned to her work.

To William he said, "I know you have much work to do, and I don't want to keep you. The last thing I want is to be a burden."

William bowed briefly and then headed outside, pausing at the door. "Violet, make sure and fetch him anything he needs," he ordered.

The girl nodded but said nothing.

When Richard was finished eating, Violet took the bowl. "Would you like some more stew?" she asked.

"Not now, thank you," Richard said, lying down and closing his eyes. The bed was narrow and uncomfortably lumpy. Something was poking him in the back, but he was almost too tired to care.

"Can I get you anything else?" Violet asked.

He opened his eyes and looked up at her. Richard's first impression had been right: She was very beautiful. She had an earnestness to her that was appealing.

"I have been away from home for a long time. Please, sit and tell me news."

Violet sat down on the chair and clasped her hands together in her lap. "What would you like to hear?" she asked with a smile.

"Everything," the prince said, closing his eyes again. He heard a door open and close as the mother exited.

"Well, the biggest news has been about your wedding."

"My what?" he asked, opening his eyes again.

"Your wedding. They say you will marry on High Feast Day, four weeks from now."

Richard groaned slightly. "Do they say to whom?"

"No, that seems something of a mystery," the girl said, and then paused, clearly hoping that he would enlighten her.

"At least they haven't chosen anyone yet," Richard remarked.

"They?"

"My parents."

"Then you have not been searching the world to find yourself a bride?" she asked inquisitively.

Her boldness was surprising to him. Neither of her parents would have dared to question him like this. Maybe she was naïve, or maybe because they were close in age she felt some sort of connection with him. Richard shifted slightly on the hard, little bed. Or maybe . . .

"This is your bed, isn't it?" he asked, opening his eyes again to try and catch her expression.

She nodded solemnly. Richard wasn't sure what he'd been expecting. If he had had a similar mishap on the way to one of the kingdoms he had visited, any of the simpering princesses would have blushed to acknowledge that he had been placed in their room. A maiden's room was private, a place where not even a father or brother would dare to disturb her.

Richard could not have told what devil suddenly possessed him, but he stared at her and asked, "You live here still because none wish to marry you?"

Violet looked at him oddly for a moment before understanding lit her eyes. Richard expected her to blush, but instead all the color drained from her face, leaving her pale and shaking with rage. Richard stared into her blazing eyes and for one moment thought that she was going to strike him. He tensed, but instead of delivering the blow Violet rose hastily to her feet, knocking over the chair.

He reached out and caught her hand, instantly sorry for what he had said. "Forgive me; I am not myself. It was a bad jest, and I should not have uttered it. No doubt you have many suitors."

She stared down at him, her limbs still shaking and her eyes flaying him alive. And in that moment something told Richard that had he not been a prince, she would have struck him.

"I am sorry, truly. I do not feel quite well, and talk of my wedding upset me."

At that, Violet seemed to relax. But she didn't move, and Richard kept hold of her hand. A long minute passed, and neither of them stirred. Finally, Violet gave a little sigh, and Richard let go of her hand. She righted the chair, then hesitated. "I should let you rest."

"Please, don't go. At least allow me to explain."

She sat slowly, warily. "Why are you so upset about your wedding?"

"You were right: I have been searching the world for a bride. However, it is my parents' choice as to which princess I shall marry. I have delivered my parents' invitation to many kings, inviting their daughters to my home. There my parents plan to test the ladies, because it is a royal decree that I marry a girl of the greatest delicacy, the greatest sensitivity."

"So, the rumors are true. There is a competition."

"Yes, I guess you could call it that. I call it abominable."

"You are a prince, though. Shouldn't the choice of a bride be yours?"

Richard laughed harshly at that. "My dear, it is because I am a prince that I can make fewer choices than a common man, fewer choices than you will have when the time comes. For princes and princesses marriage isn't about love or companionship or even family. It is about kingdoms and treaties and wars and alliances. My parents understand that. The rulers of the other kingdoms understand that."

"But Cambria is a powerful country. We don't need an alliance with another country."

"Of course we do. Other countries know how powerful we are. Some fear us, some admire us, but they're all eager to be our friends. Even the king of Lore will be sending his daughter here."

Violet paused. "But why would your parents ever consider an alliance with Lore? They attacked our country in the last war, and we crushed them."

"Yes, but that defeat was more than fifteen years ago. They have been rebuilding, and their army is larger and better equipped than ever."

"But Lorians are treacherous," Violet protested, eyes blazing.

"As my parents well know. They only took the throne when the former king and queen of Cambria were assassinated in their own castle. Assassinated by the king of Lore."

Violet paused, as if thinking that through. "I didn't know that," she said at last. "The Lorians' treachery is even deeper than I had imagined."

Richard nodded. "Yes. My parents were nobles, but that was all. The entire royal family of Cambria was murdered within an hour. My parents were the highest ranking nobles alive, and they took the throne. The outrage against the atrocity was what helped us win the war. The people of Cambria can fight like lions when wronged." He hid a smile, thinking of how she, a commoner, had nearly struck a prince who had insulted her. The spirit of Cambria was alive and well in her.

Violet pressed her hand to her forehead. "I hope you do not marry the princess of Lore. I think it would be a disgrace."

He sighed. "It would ensure peace. If I marry someone else, there is the real possibility that we shall be at war with Lore again in our lifetimes. Of course, that's true of at least half a dozen other kingdoms as well. Sometimes I think, rather than allowing me to choose a bride and risk an affront to some kingdom, my parents devised this ridiculous challenge to find the most sensitive princess."

Violet shook her head. "Well, I wish you happiness with your future bride, whomever she may be."

"Thank you," Richard replied. His head had begun to pound, and he closed his eyes once more. Within moments he was asleep.

Violet kept a watchful eye on Prince Richard as she went about her chores. He was sleeping fitfully, and occasionally he cried out. She found herself pitying him. To have so much power and yet be so powerless must be terrible! It baffled her, and she prayed that his parents might choose a wife whom he could love.

Father Paul arrived just before dinner, and when William escorted him inside, the priest's eyes widened upon seeing the figure of the prince.

"Thomas didn't tell me the patient was Prince Richard!" he exclaimed.

"We didn't know until after he had left to fetch you," William explained.

Violet helped her mother prepare dinner as Father Paul examined Richard. The prince was groggy when he awoke and seemed less clear-headed than earlier. His eyes were bright, and his cheeks were stained red.

"The wound looks good; you did a fine job of tending to it," Father Paul told Sarah. To William he added, "He seems to be getting the onset of a fever, though."

"I was afraid of that. He was out in that storm last night," William said.

"The best thing to do is make sure he has plenty of liquids and to keep him warm. I'll be back to check on him in the morning."

Sarah began to cough and moved off to a corner. Violet stared after her mother in concern. The coughing fit lasted longer than usual, and each cough seemed to shake her body like a leaf in a storm.

"Sarah, what ails you, woman?" Father Paul asked.

"I'm fine, Father," she answered, eyes watering.

He narrowed his eyes. Before he could say anything, though, Richard spoke.

"Father?"

"Yes?" Paul asked, turning his whole attention back to his patient.

"I'd appreciate it if you didn't tell anyone that I am here. This is not exactly the homecoming I had in mind," Richard muttered.

"You just rest easy, son. We'll all keep your secret as long as we can," the kindly priest assured him.

CHAPTER THREE

That night Prince Richard got worse. They did their best to keep him warm, and Violet bathed his face every half hour with a cool cloth. The fever was high, though, and he was muttering in a haze, clearly not even sure where he was. She dozed fitfully, sitting in the chair next to the bed.

In the morning, when Father Paul returned, he took one look at Richard, and the worry on his face sent a bolt of fear through Violet.

Leaving Richard in the care of the priest and her mother, Violet went to the barn to feed the horses. She was tired, and the cool air helped clear her head. Mostly, though, she needed a reprieve from the watching and waiting. Both Bessie and Baron greeted her expectantly.

"Sorry, I don't have any apples today," she said as she forked hay into their troughs. When she was finished, she leaned against Baron's stall. "He's not doing so well. Father Paul's looking after him, though. He's good at doctoring, Father Paul. He'll fix him, you'll see."

"Violet?"

She turned and saw Thomas entering the barn. "What is it?"

"Your father wants you back at the house."

She pushed off from the stall and followed Thomas back to the house in silence. Her heart sank when she saw her father waiting for her. His face was pale.

"What is it?" she asked.

"Father Paul said that as long as the fever breaks soon, Prince Richard should be all right. He says, though, that we have to watch in case his temperature drops too low. We'd have to bring it up then."

Violet nodded, but she could tell there was more. She waited, and finally her father continued.

"Your mother, she had one of her coughing spells again. She coughed up some blood. Father Paul has restricted her to her bed, and he's looking after her. You'll have to take over caring for the prince until Father Paul can make your mother well."

Violet was both frightened and relieved. It scared her that her mother's coughing was getting worse, and that now there was blood. But she was hopeful that Father Paul could heal her. "I'll do my best."

"I know you will, Daughter. You've always been a good girl."

The rest of the day Violet felt as though she were moving through a fog. She prepared simple meals of bread and cheese for herself, Thomas, and her father, but neither of the patients would take any food. She did some mending while watching her mother and Richard. Occasionally her father or Thomas would come in from the fields and allow Violet a few minutes to walk outside and stretch her legs.

When night at last came, Violet slept on a crude mattress on the floor while her father took the first turn sitting up and watching. She could hear her mother cough from time to time, but for the most part Violet managed to sleep. She didn't know what time it was when her father shook her shoulder, but Violet sat up, instantly awake.

"Your mother is sleeping just fine. The prince's fever has broken, but now he's cold as ice. Help me get him warm."

Violet nodded and took the blankets from her mattress and grabbed the extra ones that they stored in a trunk for the occasional guest or really cold weather. Together Violet and her father tucked the blankets around the prince, who was cool to the touch and shaking. He awoke groggily. "I'm so cold," he whispered.

Violet hurried to heat some broth for him and then held the bowl, helping him drink from it. William added more wood to the fire until it was a large, crackling blaze. In the light from the hearth Violet could see how tired he was. William's eyes drooped, and he swayed slightly on his feet.

"Your turn to get some sleep, Father. I'll watch him."

"Are you sure?" he asked in a hoarse whisper.

"Yes."

He hesitated for a moment before giving in. "Good, try to get him warm. Wake me if he gets worse or you need anything."

"I will," she promised.

Violet watched as her father went and lay down gently next to her mother. Sarah stirred slightly but did not waken. Within a minute Violet could tell by her father's deep breathing that he was also asleep. Then she turned all of her attention back to Prince Richard.

He was awake and looking at her. His eyes were clearer than they had been since the fever started. "Why am I so cold?" he asked her.

"Father Paul said that this might happen after your fever passed. You will be all right. See, you have lots of thick, warm blankets around you, and the fire is high."

"So cold," he said, closing his eyes.

A minute passed, and the room became warmer, but Prince Richard started shaking harder. Violet laid a hand on his forehead, and it was like touching ice. She rubbed her hands hard together until they were hot and then placed them on his face, willing the warmth from her skin into his. He murmured slightly.

A memory came to her. Once as a child she had been sick and so very cold. Her parents had put her in their bed, laying her between them with the blankets over them all. Violet remembered how the heat from their bodies had warmed her when the fire and the blankets had not. She stared down at Richard. She had promised her father that she would keep him warm.

Violet lifted the blankets and lay down on her bed. She tucked the blankets around them both and then wrapped her body around him. He shivered and then turned toward her.

She lay still, trying to quiet the pounding of her heart. Violet had never been so close to a man. She could feel his breath on her cheek. After a while she could feel warmth returning to his skin, and she began to relax. She dozed fitfully.

Just before dawn she finally rose. Prince Richard was sleeping deeply, and his skin no longer felt cold to the touch. Her father was standing in front of the fireplace eating a piece of bread.

William gestured toward the door, and they walked outside. "How is he?" William asked, once they were clear of the house.

"He stopped shivering a little while ago. He seems to be warm again, and he's sleeping. How's Mother?"

"Sleeping as well. I think they both had a lot more sleep than either of us," he said, smiling briefly.

Violet stopped by the barn to check on the horses before returning to the house. Inside she was startled to find Richard awake and sitting up. Her mother was also stirring.

"Well, now that everyone's awake, we can have breakfast," Violet said cheerfully.

Richard watched closely as Violet made breakfast. He was feeling better, stronger. He vividly remembered resting beside her, shivering and clinging to her warmth. He was beginning to think that she might be the greatest mystery he had ever encountered.

The priest arrived shortly after they had finished eating. "I'm relieved to see you looking so well," he told Richard.

"So am I," Richard answered.

The priest examined him closely, then sat back with a satisfied look. "I'd say you should be fit to travel the day after tomorrow. By then you should have regained your strength sufficiently."

Paul then turned his attention to Sarah, and Violet approached Richard.

"Are you feeling better, then?" Violet asked.

"Yes. In fact I could use a bit of fresh air. Would you care to accompany me outside?"

"Yes, Highness."

His legs were stiff, but Richard suspected they would be fine once he was able to stretch them a bit. Outside the house he lifted his face to the warmth of the sun and breathed in deeply of the fresh air. It seemed as though he could actually feel his strength returning to him.

He turned toward the barn, wanting to see for

himself that Baron was all right. Violet walked beside him with a sure step. He glanced at her, admiring the way that she carried herself. There was no self-conscious preening on her part, only the strong, steady stride of someone who had spent her life working outdoors instead of confined to a room doing stitchery. It was refreshing, and so different from anything he had ever known as to be novel.

Baron greeted Richard enthusiastically, and Richard stroked his nose, relieved to see his companion uninjured. "That was a nasty spill we took, boy. I'm just glad you seem to be in better shape than me."

To Violet he said, "Thank you for looking after him."

"It was no hardship," she answered. "He's a good horse, and he'll stand still for anything if there is the promise of an apple."

Richard laughed appreciatively. "Hear that, Baron? She understands you better than most."

Violet flushed at that, and the pink in her tan cheeks made her look all the lovelier.

Violet spent the rest of the day showing Richard around the farm. He had to stop and rest often, but each time he would get up with a dogged determination. Richard slept soundly that night, but Violet tossed and turned on her makeshift mattress, trying not to count the number of times her mother coughed.

With the new dawn Richard was up as early as she was, eager to walk more. They walked slowly out to where he had had his accident and then rested themselves in the shade of a tree growing by the stream.

"Tell me about your travels," she urged, curious to hear of the world beyond her own.

"There was one castle that was perched high on the top of a mountain. It took three days to climb up to it, and when we arrived, it was like a snowy wonderland. The flowers were blooming despite the snow, and the blossoms were of purple and blue and yellow."

"And was there a princess there?" she asked.

He laughed. "Yes. She was a very delicate creature, no taller than this," Richard said, standing and indicating a line just below his chest.

Violet stood up and found that she was a good deal taller, for the top of her head reached his chin.

"I thought that a good, stiff wind would carry her away," he said, laughing.

Violet laughed too, at the thought of it. "Surely she was too delicate!" she exclaimed, trying to picture the girl in her head.

"Wait, there was another, in a castle deep in a valley surrounded by rivers. She was so thin, it was as though you could see through her," he said, eyes sparkling with laughter.

"What happened?" Violet asked excitedly, sensing there was more to the story.

"We went for a walk in the gardens, and while we were talking, a rose petal fell and bruised her foot so terribly that the poor thing couldn't walk for three days."

"A rose petal?" Violet asked, bewildered. "Are you making fun?"

"No, I wish I was. Poor dear. I don't know how she'll ever survive the carriage ride here."

Violet started laughing.

"And what has amused you so?" Richard asked.

"How would a woman like that ever manage to bear you children? She would probably faint at the very thought. If you so much as kissed her, you would probably knock loose all her teeth." Violet continued laughing so hard that she began to cry. A strange look passed over Richard's face, and she couldn't tell if he was going to rebuke her or begin laughing as well.

"I can assure you I am not so rough and crude a kisser," he said at last.

"I did not mean to imply you were," she said, trying to wipe the tears from her face. "I only meant that the princess is so frail it's a wonder her own clothes don't crush her with their weight; an embrace might crack her bones. And if she was ever kissed by a farm boy, the force would probably kill her."

"So, farm boys are forceful kissers," the prince said, musingly.

"Aye. They wouldn't know any other way."

"And what of farm girls?"

"They wouldn't know any other way, either," Violet said, smiling and blushing all at once.

Richard moved like lightning, his left arm wrapping around Violet's waist and his right hand cupping the back of her head. His face moved in toward hers, and Violet cried out in alarm. She was afraid, for she could feel the power of him, the roughness. But at the last instant, when Richard's lips met hers, it was whisper soft. Not hard and fierce as she had imagined. Though his lips were barely touching hers, Violet could feel the strength of him wrapped around her. He swept her backward, supporting her body with his arm and her head with his hand, and still his kiss was gentle like a spring breeze and playful as a kitten. It overwhelmed her. She succumbed to it completely, letting herself go limp in his arms. Richard's lips were soft, teasing, with a promise of something more to come. And then, slowly, he lifted her up, set her back upon her feet, and pulled away.

"What was that for?" she asked, her voice and body shaking from the onslaught.

"That is so that you shall know the difference," Richard said, his breathing ragged.

"But what good does that do me?" Violet burst out, bewildered. "I'm as likely to teach a pig to dance as teach a boy from the village to kiss like that."

"Then take it as a token, a thank-you for all that you have done for me."

"I would have done it for a starving beggar, let alone the man whose family owns the land my family works," she said.

Something dark and inscrutable shadowed his face. "I'm sorry. I'm sure the other night you would have been happier tending to a beggar."

With that, Violet slapped him, hard and fast across the face. She gasped, realizing what she had done. Prince Richard bent down to gaze at her fiercely, and Violet's heart thudded, as she expected him to denounce her for her crime.

It was the slap Richard had expected from her days before, and even as it stung his cheek, he realized that he deserved it. Something about her brought out the devil in him. He wasn't sure why, but he knew that before he left her and the farm the following morning there was something he needed to hear from her.

"That first day, when I woke up, before I asked you your name, you asked, 'Is it you?' What did you mean by that?"

Violet blushed fiercely and turned her face away from him, looking to the grass at their feet. "Nothing," she answered shortly. "You must have been delirious."

"No, I didn't yet have the fever, and I remember clearly my conversation with you and your father. I heard what you asked. What did it mean?" he pressed.

Violet turned and started walking toward the house. "I'm hungry. We should go eat lunch."

Richard caught her by the arm and spun her around to face him, his curiosity raging out of control. "Did you recognize me? Had we met? Were you asking if I was the prince?"

"Yes, that was it," she stammered, though she refused to meet his eyes.

"You are lying to me," he said, surprised that she

would be so daring and even more surprised that it mattered to him. Richard took a deep breath and then, using the very voice he used to command lesser nobles to do his bidding, he ordered, "Tell me what you truly meant."

The wind picked up around them and blew Violet's hair back from her face so that it stood out nearly straight. Richard felt the wind's cold fingers plucking at him, but he stood rooted to the ground, waiting for her answer.

Finally, she looked up at him, and her great violet eyes met his. "It's just a game I've played for a couple of years now. Whenever my eyes meet those of a man my age, I wonder if he's going to be the one I'll marry. It was just habit. I wondered the same about you, before I knew who you were. When you were just a nameless stranger lying in my bed. I never meant to say anything out loud."

Richard's heart began to pound, hard and savage. He leaned closer to stare more deeply into her eyes. His mouth had gone dry. All this time he had been searching the world over for his bride, and this girl had been searching this village for her groom. It seemed impossible that they should have met, but they had. Was it fate?

When he spoke, it was no more than a whisper. "Is it me?" Richard asked. Their faces were only inches apart, and the question shimmered in the air between them. He forgot to breathe, waiting for what she might say. But Violet just stared up at him with eyes that could consume a man's soul.

Her lips parted, and she seemed about to speak. A sudden shout caused them both to jump. Violet stepped away from him.

Her father stood waving his hat in the doorway of the house.

Richard thought he saw a tear trickle down her cheek, but he realized it was a raindrop when one hit his brow.

"Father Paul must be here," Violet said, her voice strained. Then she picked up her skirts and ran toward the house.

He followed, watching the sway of her golden hair. What had she been about to say? Somehow Richard had the feeling that he would never know.

Suddenly Violet stopped. He could tell she was staring off in the distance toward the castle. He followed the line of her vision and saw the storm clouds rapidly spreading from that direction. Another drop of rain fell, heavier than the first, followed by another and then another.

The storm came, sudden and unexpected. Violet and Richard barely made it inside before the lightning started. Violet stood at the window, shivering as she stared out into the darkening afternoon.

The priest was tending to her mother, and Sarah seemed worse than the day before. While Father Paul was talking with William, Richard came and stood beside Violet, staring out at the rain.

"Do you care for me?" he asked, his voice low enough that only she could hear.

"Would it matter?" Violet asked.

He hesitated, as if looking for the right words.

She plunged in, fear and bitterness tugging at her hushed voice. "No, it wouldn't," she answered for him. "It's not about you or me; it's about kingdoms and treaties and wars and alliances. You said so yourself."

Richard seemed to have no answer, for he turned away, retreating to the center of the room. Violet could hear her father, the priest, and Richard talking together in low tones, but she continued to stare out the window.

When Violet went to bed that night, she couldn't sleep for many hours. Everything seemed to be happening so quickly that she couldn't make sense of it. She thought of the conversation with Richard, about the princesses he had met, and she felt a sharp pang as she wondered which would be his wife. She thought about the kiss, and her lips burned with the memory of it. There was so much to take in. And then there was the storm, so soon on the heels of the first. Violet drifted off to sleep, fear curling around her heart. In the morning, when she awoke, everything had changed.

CHAPTER FOUR

As soon as she opened her eyes, Violet knew something was wrong. The air was cold, and she reached for a shawl as she sat up. Shivering, she wrapped it around herself before shrugging off her blanket and standing up. She found her father sitting at the table, his head in his hands. She glanced around the room. Richard wasn't there and in her heart, she knew he was gone. Violet's eyes fell on her parents' bed, and a chill settled on her as she saw her mother's still form.

"Mother?" Violet whispered.

Her father looked up at her, and she could see that he had been crying. "There's nothing more Father Paul can do."

Tears stung her eyes. "How long?" Violet asked, her voice shaking.

"Could be anytime."

Her mother stirred, and Violet pulled a chair up next to the bed. Her mother opened her eyes and looked at her. "There's something you need to know," she said, her breathing ragged and her face pinched in pain.

"Don't try to talk; just rest," Violet urged. "You need your strength to get better."

She shook her head. "I'm dying, Violet, and I need to tell you the truth before I do."

Violet felt the tears sliding down her cheeks. "What is it, Mother?"

"That's just it," Sarah whispered. "I'm not your mother."

Richard's heart was heavy as he rode up to the castle. He had left in the dark hour before dawn, without rousing Violet. William had seen him off, and he'd left the man with a few coins and the warmest thanks. It had been a cowardly act, but Richard hadn't trusted himself to say good-bye to Violet.

She was amazing. She was strong yet graceful, intelligent and compassionate. She was everything he would want in a wife and nothing that his parents would accept. "Violet, why couldn't you have been a princess?" Richard whispered to the wind, wondering if it would carry his words to her.

While it had rained lightly throughout most of the morning, the sun shone weakly in the sky. Richard could tell from the look of the dark clouds on the horizon, though, that it was only a temporary respite from the storm. It looked like he would beat the rest of it as he drew close to the castle.

A cry went up from the watchtower as the guards recognized him and his horse. The sound used to thrill him, but this time Richard squared his shoulders with a groan. He was home, which meant that in a few weeks' time he would be married off to some useless girl of his parents' choosing. He touched his heels to Baron, and they cantered into the courtyard.

No sooner had he reined the horse to a stop and dismounted than princesses seemed to pour out of every doorway, calling and waving to him. Amidst the noise and confusion his father suddenly appeared, a smile on his face, and wrapped his arm around him.

"Welcome home, son. I see you've found a wife."

Richard could feel his heart sink. "Which one?" he asked.

"I don't know, but we'll figure that out soon enough."

Richard looked around. He saw the girl whose foot had been bruised by the rose petal. She looked like she was going to faint from the overexertion of the moment. One of the other girls jostled her, and she cried out in anguish. Prince Richard shook his head. All of the princesses vied for his attention except for one. He recognized her from the mountaintop castle. She was so small in stature as to be remarkable, and she stood back from the group, a look of vague interest on her face, but nothing more. Richard sighed. At least she had some dignity, and he found himself hoping she would beat out the others.

"Can we speak in private?" he asked his father.

The king nodded. "Your mother wants to see you first."

"I've missed you both," Richard admitted. He took a deep breath. "And the three of us need to talk."

When the three of them were seated in his parents' chambers, with greetings exchanged and servants dismissed, Richard took a deep breath. "I found the woman I want to marry."

His parents both looked surprised. "Which girl is she?" his mother asked.

"She's not here."

"When do you expect her to arrive?" his father asked.

"Actually, I'm not expecting her to arrive at all."

"Who is she?" the queen asked, her blue eyes sparkling intently. It was strange—with her porcelain skin, black hair, and blue eyes she looked nothing like Violet, and yet in some strange way he found similarities in them. He shook his head, wondering if because he loved her, he would always see Violet in every woman he knew.

"Her name is Violet. Her father works a farm half a day's ride from here, and she saved my life."

"I think you'd better start from the beginning," the king said.

Richard looked at his father. The king was several inches taller than him, with dark brown hair and a beard that always made him look like a lion. Richard had been told that while he had his mother's looks, he had his father's bearing. He took a deep breath and drew himself up to his full height before beginning to tell them about the last few days.

When he reached the conclusion, he stood, trying not to betray his agitation over what their response would be. They were both silent for a moment, and then his father cleared his throat.

"Richard, grateful as we are to this young lady and her parents, we cannot allow you to marry her."

In his heart Richard had known that was how his father would respond, but he couldn't control the anger that rose in him. "She is a stronger and nobler woman than any of the simpering princesses that are in this castle," he said.

"That might be, but you know that you have to marry a princess. We need a strong alliance with another kingdom," his mother said.

"We also need to solidify our position here," his father said.

Richard wished with all his heart that the old monarchs hadn't been assassinated. Then he would be only a nobleman, not a prince, and he could have married the girl he wanted.

"I'm sorry," his father continued. "But it must be a princess. Now that you're here, the competition will begin tomorrow."

"And what exactly is this competition of yours going to entail?" Richard asked through gritted teeth.

"Six distinct challenges testing the sensitivity and nature of each princess. The princess who passes all the challenges will be your bride."

His fate sealed, Richard took his leave of his parents and headed for his room. He was halfway there when he heard joyous barking and turned to see a dog racing down the hall toward him.

"Duke!"

The dog leaped into his arms and licked his face, forcing him to laugh. "I missed you too, boy."

Together they continued to Richard's chambers. A giant four-poster bed dominated the bedroom area. Furs covered the stone floors, and tapestries that had been woven commemorating the defeat of Lore graced the walls. He stood in front of the one that depicted the slaughter of the old king and queen. He had often stared at it, the royal family in their chamber, eyes wide in death. To the left, soldiers of Lore were leaving the room. To the right, several people stood grieving: servants, a woman with a child, soldiers. He and his parents featured prominently among the mourners. He turned away; the past couldn't be changed, and apparently neither could his future.

He looked around and thought about the long year that he'd been gone. So many things he had seen and done, and yet here he was again, seemingly no wiser or bolder than when he had left.

I should have forced the priest to marry Violet and me. If I had brought her home as my wife, there would have been nothing my parents could do. For one wild moment Richard thought about slipping away and going back to her. Slinking away like a cur in the night wasn't exactly courageous, though.

He was tired. It had been a long journey, and his head ached as though to remind him that he was still recovering from his injury. He sank down on his bed and wondered what new horrors awaited him in the coming weeks. Duke just whined and licked his hand.

Violet stared at her mother in disbelief. "Why would you say such a thing?" she asked, wondering if the illness had affected Sarah's mind.

"Because it's the truth, and it is long past time that you knew it."

Her father rose from his chair and came to stand behind Violet. He put his hand on her shoulder, and she looked up at him. "Your mother is speaking the truth."

"Are you my real father?" Violet asked.

"No, but I couldn't love you any more if I were."

"Then who are my parents?"

"We're not entirely sure," he said.

Violet stared at one and then the other in disbelief. "Was I a foundling? Did you discover me in the forest like some fairy child?"

The idea was absurd, but no more absurd to her than the thought that the people she loved so dearly were not her parents.

William sighed deeply and then sat on the edge of the bed. He took his wife's hand in his, and together they looked at Violet.

"Seventeen years ago we were at war with Lore," William said.

"I know. The Feasting is when we celebrate our victory."

"For many months it wasn't certain that we would win. The turning point of the war came during one of the fiercest storms anyone could remember," Sarah said.

A storm. Of course. For one wild moment she wondered if maybe it wasn't her fortunes alone that were tied to the tempests, but those of the entire kingdom.

"Assassins entered the castle in the middle of the night under the cover of the storm and murdered the royal family as they slept," William said.

Violet nodded, still not sure where they were going with the story. "And the outrage brought on by the atrocity was what spurred the people of Cambria to ultimate victory."

"Yes," William said.

"How does any of this relate to you not being my real parents?"

"In the hours before dawn, before anyone knew what had happened at the castle, we were woken by someone pounding on the door," Sarah said. She paused and coughed a couple of times, each one sounding more painful than the last. She finally stopped, but her eyes were watering, and there was blood on the kerchief she was holding.

William squeezed Sarah's hand, the pain in his eyes almost unbearable. "It's okay, Mother. I can tell it."

Sarah nodded and closed her eyes for a moment as if to gather her strength.

"A woman was standing outside in the storm," William continued. "She had a baby with her, a little girl less than a month old, with the most beautiful violet-colored eyes."

Violet began to shake.

"The woman said her name was Eve and that she was your nurse, and she begged us to take you in, to keep you safe, and to never tell anyone where you had come from. She said that men might come looking for you, to kill you. We offered you both shelter from the storm. You were so tiny, so helpless. We agreed to take care of you, but Eve refused to stay and was gone soon after. She promised to return when it was safe, if she could. We never saw her again, though."

"And did men come looking for me?"

"Yes. They were soldiers of Lore. They claimed that they were looking for a kidnapped child. They tried to pretend they were Cambrians, but we knew they were not. The men arrived not an hour after the woman had left."

"And you told them that I was your child?"

"We did indeed, and they believed us and left. The next day we had word about the tragedy at the castle, that all the royal family had been killed: the king, the queen, two young princes, and a baby girl three weeks of age. There were rumors, however, that the girl's body wasn't found."

Violet gasped. "A baby girl! That could have been me."

"We have loved you and raised you as our own. But we have long suspected that you were the infant princess, saved by a nursemaid and hidden from all."

"Is this true?" Violet asked, turning to look at her mother.

Sarah nodded and then reached out her arms and folded Violet into an embrace.

"Why are you telling me all this now?"

"We should have told you years ago, but we were selfish, afraid we'd lose you," William said.

Violet began to weep. "That could never have happened."

"When the war was over, we were afraid how the new king and queen would react if they discovered the rightful heir was alive. They might have taken you from us, or worse."

A chill danced up Violet's spine. Had she escaped death and never known it?

"But now you must go to the castle," Sarah said, her voice weaker.

Violet shook her head. "I don't want to be a princess or a queen. I just want to be your daughter. The king and queen have gotten along fine all these years. There's nothing I could do for them, nothing I could offer."

"It's not them that we're thinking of," William said quietly.

"The boy loves you," her mom said.

Violet blushed. "He barely knows me."

"He knows enough. It's possible to fall in love all in a moment. Your father and I did," Sarah said, smiling gently at her husband.

"And you love him," William said.

Violet lowered her eyes. "Even if I did care for him, he must marry a princess."

"Child, that's what we've been trying to tell you," her father said. "You *are* a princess."

"I'm a princess," she whispered slowly.

Her mother's face was filled with pain, and she was having a hard time breathing, but she smiled at Violet and said, "Now, go get your prince."

"But I can't leave you, not when you're—"

Sarah shushed her. "I will live as long as I am supposed to live, and your being here won't change that one way or the other. But I need to know that you're fulfilling your destiny and fighting for your happiness."

An hour later, with her mother's words ringing in her ears, Violet was in the barn saddling up Bessie with her father's help. At the last, William held the horse's head as Violet swung up onto her back.

"Mother?" Violet asked.

He shook his head. "She's slipping away from us."

"I should stay."

"No. I know she doesn't want you to remember her this way. Go and bring back a prince I can call my son."

She leaned down and kissed his cheek. "I'm so frightened, Father," she whispered.

"I know," he said. "But it's only change, lass."

"Will you send word?" she asked.

"When it's over, I'll come to the castle to see you outride, outcook, and outsmart all those other princesses."

Violet smiled sadly. Somehow she didn't think she would be so lucky as to be allowed to compete with the others in those areas. She turned Bessie's head toward the barn doors and urged the mare out into the storm.

It took only a few seconds before she was drenched through to the skin. Her mind was torn between thoughts of her adoptive mother lying on her deathbed and the man that she loved marrying another. When the tears came, Violet let them fall freely, the storm without raging as the storm within gathered force.

As they entered the village, Bessie turned toward the small marketplace she was accustomed to visiting. Violet gently pulled Bessie's head back around and aimed the horse's nose toward the hill in the distance. The rain had eased, and she could actually see the castle perched there in the pale sunlight that filtered through the clouds.

Violet felt a thrill of excitement exiting the village. When she reached the castle, she would be farther from home than she could ever remember traveling. Though, if what her parents had said was true, she had been far from home all along.

A blast of cold wind presaged the arrival of more rain. Violet urged Bessie into a trot just as the skies opened again and water cascaded down on them. The mare tossed her head, and Violet put a steadying hand on her neck. "Easy, girl, we have to keep going."

The intensity of the storm doubled, and a fierce

wind began to blow as if seeking to force them to turn back. Fear began to overtake her. Maybe she was making a mistake; maybe she should return home. Her parents needed her. *What about Richard?* a voice in her head whispered.

Maybe he doesn't care for me like I think he does. What if it was all a mistake, and he rejects me? Maybe his parents have already chosen a princess for him, and I'll have to watch him marry someone else. Who am I, after all, but just a farm girl who helped him? He may have been grateful, but perhaps gratitude was all that he felt. She thought about the kiss they had shared. Could he have kissed her like that if he felt nothing for her? The wind stung her cheeks and blew wet locks of hair into her eyes. Violet gritted her teeth, crouched low on Bessie's back, and urged the mare forward.

It was not long before the castle loomed ahead of Violet in the darkness, the rain bouncing and sliding off its massive stones. She rode into a courtyard and then slid off Bessie's back, panting with exhaustion and shivering with the cold.

"Milady, let me assist you," a guard said, running up to her. Another man appeared and began to lead Bessie away.

"I've come to see the king and queen," Violet said, shocked at her own audacity. Still, it was too late to turn back.

"Then you must come in out of the rain."

She set her jaw, stilling the fluttering in her heart, and strode forward into the castle.

"Perhaps my lady would like to refresh herself," the guard suggested.

Another servant scurried forward to take charge of her, and the guard bowed and returned to his duties. The man looked her up and down with a disapproving look on his face. Even though he was a servant, his clothes were finer than any Violet had ever seen in the village.

She looked around and could see the sheer size of the castle sprawling beyond the room in which she stood. The stone floors were lined with fresh rushes, and the air was warm and perfumed. She could see a massive hearth in the room beyond with a fire crackling in it.

"I'm a princess, and I'm here to see the king and queen," she said, returning her attention to the servant.

"Very good, milady. We shall just make you comfortable, and I will arrange an audience for you later."

Violet shook her head. If she didn't speak to them now, she might never find the courage to confront Richard's parents. "I will see them now," she said, hoping that her voice held an air of authority to it.

The conviction in her voice must have been clear, because the man bowed and gestured for her to follow. A minute later Violet paused outside a large room where she could see many people milling about within. Just below the ceiling dozens of flags hung; she recognized the flag of Cambria and then the one of Lore. She bristled in anger when she saw it and then forced herself to take a deep breath as she realized that the flags were probably representative of every royal family in attendance at the castle for the competition.

"Milady, how shall I announce you?" the man asked, turning to her with lifted brow.

She hesitated for a moment, wondering what she should say. "Violet," she said at last.

For a moment she thought she saw the man smirk, but then he sailed into the room, and she could see him walk toward the thrones. She couldn't hear what he was saying, but when he turned toward her, she realized that must be her invitation to enter.

"Courage," she whispered to herself. Violet walked into the room. Courtiers and servants stood about in small groups talking. At the end of the room was a raised dais with three elaborately carved wooden thrones on it. The legs of each were carved as standing lions, and a deep, rich purple material covered the seats and backs.

From his place on his throne Richard caught sight of Violet and leaned forward. Her heart began to pound. Richard blinked a couple of times, brow furrowed, and then his eyes widened in recognition. With great effort Violet wrenched her eyes from his gaze and turned to look at the king and queen as she halted before them and clumsily curtsied.

The queen's eyes widened in surprise as she took in Violet's bedraggled appearance. A moment later the woman looked perfectly restrained again, like nothing could shake her.

"Violet," Richard said, in strangled tones.

His mother glanced sharply at him, and Violet realized that the queen knew who she was.

"Child, why have you come out in this storm?" the king asked in a mild tone.

"Your Majesty, I have come to compete for your son's hand in marriage," Violet said.

"Richard, this is your farm girl?" the queen asked.

"Yes, she's the one," Richard said.

Violet realized that the room had grown quiet as everyone stopped talking. She could feel that all eyes were on her.

The king cleared his throat. "So, we have you to thank for the safe return of our son?" he asked.

Violet glanced at Richard, who was nodding his head. She hadn't been the only one to care for the prince. Her parents and Father Paul had aided him as well. Still, from the look in Richard's eyes she could tell this was no time for her to be humble. "Yes," Violet said.

"My dear, we owe a debt of gratitude to your family for caring for our son while he was ill. We would like to reward you. However, only a princess can enter the competition," the king said, his voice still gentle.

"And a princess stands before you," Violet said, raising her chin.

CHAPTER FIVE

The king and queen both stared at Violet for what seemed like an eternity. Violet stood in her drenched and filthy clothes, water dripping from her brow and rolling off the tip of her nose, and tried to act as dignified as she could despite the circumstances.

The king and queen wore dark blue robes shot through with gold, and crowns that glistened with gemstones of every hue. They both seemed so composed, so sure of themselves, of who they were and what that meant. They were everything she wasn't.

There were murmurs from the others in the room, but Violet kept her eyes fixed on Richard and his parents. The king and queen glanced at each other, and even though they didn't speak, Violet knew that they were communicating with their eyes, just as her parents had always done. Violet glanced at Richard. What would it be like to know someone so well that you could read the tiniest, most subtle emotions on his face?

"You say you are a princess?" the queen asked, turning back to Violet.

"I believe that to be true, yes," Violet said, heart beating faster.

"Can you explain yourself?" the king requested.

"My mother is dying," Violet said, voice cracking slightly. Tears slid down her already damp cheeks. She didn't dare look at Richard, who had met her mother, nor at the queen, who was Richard's mother. Instead she focused on his father. "On her deathbed she revealed to me that I was not her true daughter. A nursemaid brought me to my parents' farm as an infant and asked my parents to keep me safe. The nursemaid said that people would be looking for me and—if they found me—would try to kill me."

"Because you were a princess?" the king asked, leaning forward sharply.

Violet nodded.

"Did this nursemaid have a name?" the queen asked.

"Eve."

Again the king and queen exchanged looks, and then both sat back on their thrones. "Thank you for sharing your story. We will investigate your claim," the king said. "For now, because this tournament would not have come to pass if you had not saved our son, we will allow you to compete."

Violet couldn't decide whether to shout for joy or

collapse in exhaustion. Instead she forced herself to bow and say in as calm a voice as she could manage, "Thank you, Your Majesties."

The king waved forward one of the female servants who was standing nearby. "June, please show the lady Violet to a room."

Violet bowed again. Richard looked at her and smiled in a way that made her blush. She turned and followed June out of the hall.

As Violet followed June down a corridor, June turned to her apologetically. "Unfortunately, you'll be sharing a room with another princess. So many young ladies have arrived, and half of them accompanied by parents or relatives; we don't have rooms for all."

Violet smiled, thinking of the small house that she shared with her parents. "I don't have any problem sharing," she said.

The two climbed a grand staircase and turned down a long hallway lined with doors. Violet wondered briefly if she would get lost among so many rooms. June turned into the open door at the far end of the corridor.

Violet followed the servant into the room. The bedroom was grand, and indeed larger than her entire house. A girl about Violet's age was seated in a chair looking quizzically at her. She was beautiful, with auburn hair and large green eyes. "Princess Genevieve, Princess Violet," June said with a curtsy to the other girl in the room.

"Hello," Genevieve said, rising from the chair.

"Hello," Violet said, trying not to smile when she realized how tiny the other girl was. She couldn't help but wonder if she was the one Richard had said was so short.

"Miladies, the banquet will be in one hour," June said before leaving.

"Where are your things?" Genevieve asked.

Violet looked down at her sodden dress. "I'm afraid this is all I have," she said, ruefully. Violet braced herself, expecting Genevieve to laugh at her.

Instead Genevieve's eyes flew open wide. "What an adventure you must have had! How long did it take you to get here?"

"My whole life, it seems," Violet answered frankly.

"How exciting! You must tell me all about it," Genevieve said, eyes flashing with excitement and alabaster skin flushing. She clapped her hands together like a child receiving a longed-for gift.

"Gladly," Violet said.

Just then a trio of servants bustled into the room and seized Genevieve. "My lady, we must get you ready for the banquet!" one exclaimed.

"Now, you haven't been agitating yourself, have you?" another asked.

"You know what your mother would say," the third added.

Genevieve's face fell. Violet watched in fascination as the three women hurried Genevieve into a fresh dress and began brushing her hair. Violet shook her head in amazement when Genevieve's protests of wanting to brush her own hair went unheeded.

Genevieve looked so forlorn that Violet's heart went out to her.

"I wish I could loan you a dress to wear tonight," Genevieve said.

"I don't think I could wear any of yours," Violet said.

Genevieve shook her head. "Where are your servants?" Genevieve asked, scowling briefly at her own.

"I don't have any."

"Then who will help you get ready?"

Before Violet could answer, Genevieve said brightly, "Christine can help you." She indicated the youngest of the three servants.

"There'll be none of that," one of the other women spoke up. "It will be our hides if you aren't presentable."

Genevieve's face fell. But a movement in the doorway caused her eyes to light up.

"Milady?"

Violet turned around and saw an older lady standing just inside the door holding a gown of pale green. It was the loveliest thing Violet had ever seen.

"Milady?" the woman repeated, and with a start Violet realized she was speaking to her.

"Yes?"

"I was instructed to bring you this gown."

"It's for me?" Violet whispered in awe.

"It is."

Violet took the dress, marveling at the feel of the fabric beneath her fingertips. The woman gave her a small nod and then turned and left. Genevieve managed to free herself and came over to look at it. The green was so deep that it reminded Violet of the forest glistening under a winter sun. Delicate gold embroidery circled the neck and wrists in a pattern that reminded Violet of vines.

"It's beautiful," Violet said.

"It's very expensive."

"I've never seen anything so pretty."

"It isn't yours?"

"No," Violet said.

"Well, someone wants you to be the most exquisite lady in the castle."

Violet shook her head. "It must be some mistake, or else maybe they didn't want me wearing this to dinner," she said, indicating her current dress.

"It would reflect badly on all of us," Genevieve noted. "Still, I think whoever sent you this dress must be very fond of you."

Violet thought of Richard. Could it have been him? He was the only one she knew in the castle, after all. "Maybe so," she said.

She glanced down at herself. "I just wish they'd been fond enough to send shoes as well," she said regretfully, but with a hint of humor.

Genevieve glanced down at Violet's tattered slippers. "You can wear a pair of mine."

Violet shook her head. "I don't think they'd fit."

"Actually, I think we wear the same size."

Violet glanced down and noticed that Genevieve's feet were much larger than she had expected.

"Christine, please bring me a pair of slippers," Genevieve said.

With a disapproving cluck at Violet, Christine handed over the slippers. They were black, and soft to the touch and larger than she would have expected. Black beading covered much of the toes. Violet took them and then sat in a chair to try them on.

"My brother always teases me and asks me when I'm going to grow into my feet," Genevieve said as Violet slid on the shoes.

The slippers fit perfectly. Violet admired them for a moment, hoping that the dress would fit so well.

She looked at the rest of her and realized that she really needed to wash before putting on the dress. She found a washbasin and pitcher and set about cleaning up.

As it turned out, the dress was also a perfect fit. Genevieve loaned her a brush, and Violet managed to braid her wet hair into a single rope down her back. After a few minutes work Violet checked her reflection in a looking glass.

"I look like a princess," she whispered in awe.

"I would hope so," Genevieve teased, her demeanor relaxing now that she was no longer being fussed over by her servants. "Let's go; we don't want to be the last to arrive."

Out in the corridor they found themselves swept

into a procession. Young women poured from every room to join the throng heading for the main hall. Arrayed in so many different colors, heads bobbing about, they made Violet think of them as a field of wildflowers waving gently in the breeze, all consumed by a single thought: Which one of them would be deemed worthy to be Prince Richard's bride?

They descended the staircase, and Violet tried to get a good look at the girls around her. From what she saw, Genevieve was certainly one of the prettiest ones. Violet ran a hand over her hair, wondering how she compared and sure that she stood out as the outsider in the group.

I don't belong here, she thought, her stomach twisting in knots. When Violet reached the bottom of the staircase, she paused, watching as the others continued into the hall. Even though the king and queen had let her enter the competition, Violet didn't have a prayer of winning. She looked at the other girls, with their petite figures, pale skin, and soft hands, and she knew she was nothing like them. She was fooling herself if she thought she could pass for a princess, let alone a delicate, sensitive one. Why should she try if she was destined to fail?

Genevieve glanced back, but Violet waved her on. "Hello."

Startled, Violet turned. She found herself staring into Richard's eyes.

"Hello," she said, her voice a bit unsteady.

"I'm sorry I frightened you."

"No, it's all right."

"You look amazing," Richard said.

Violet smiled. "Thank you for the dress."

He shook his head. "I didn't send it for you, although I wish I had thought of it," he confessed.

"If it wasn't you who sent the dress, then who did?"

"I honestly don't know. But if I find out, I'll be sure to thank them."

A beautiful dog with long reddish-gold hair bounded up next to Richard and whined. "Hey, Duke, let me introduce you to the lady Violet."

Violet extended her hand, and the dog sniffed it and then licked it. "He's beautiful," she said.

"Thanks," Richard replied. He paused, then continued, "I'm sorry to hear about your mother's health. She's a wonderful woman. Is there anything I can do?"

Violet felt the smile fade from her lips. "Father Paul is doing the best anyone can. Thank you, but I don't think anything can be done."

Violet searched Richard's eyes. There were so many things she wanted to say. The hallway became silent as the last of the chattering princesses disappeared from view. They were alone. Violet could tell him exactly how she felt, but somehow being in the castle was so much more awkward than walking around the farm.

The grand size of the building took her breath away, and she had been almost afraid to look at the tapestries that decorated the walls, feeling as though a stare might ruin the delicate embroideries. At home they had to make things that would last and survive heavy use.

"I'm not quite sure why I'm here," Violet blurted out. She had to talk to someone, and she didn't think Genevieve would understand. At any rate, even if Genevieve might understand, it would mean explaining a lot more than Violet was in the mood to explain at the moment.

Richard stepped closer, and for a moment Violet forgot to breathe. He put a finger under her chin and tilted her head up toward his face. "There's a question I asked you that you've never answered."

He pinned her with his stare, and Violet felt the rest of the world melt away. It was as if only the two of them existed. Softly, he asked, "Is it me?"

"Yes," she breathed.

Richard smiled and leaned in to Violet. She closed her eyes.

"Your Highness!"

Violet jerked, and she opened her eyes just in time to see Richard turn aside, a look of irritation on his face. The servant she had met earlier stood there, his eyebrows arched with vague disapproval. "Your parents wish for you to join them in the throne room."

"Thank you, Steward," Richard nodded. So the man was the steward, the one in charge of running the castle. No wonder he looked at her disapprovingly.

When Richard turned to excuse himself, he stared

at Violet with smoldering eyes. "Pardon me," he said, bowing. "I'll see you at the banquet."

Violet nodded, not trusting herself to speak. Prince Richard strode toward the throne room after the steward, and after a moment Violet continued on in the direction the other girls had gone and quickly entered the great hall.

In the banquet hall Violet discovered that Genevieve had saved her a seat toward the head of the table, and she gratefully took it. Violet counted eighteen girls besides herself at the table. There were several others that she took to be parents or older siblings of some of the princesses.

"Did you come here with anyone in addition to your servants?" Violet asked.

Genevieve wrinkled her nose. "My cousin—he's the one over there with the red beard," she said, inclining her head to the left.

Violet saw that he was flirting with several ladies in his vicinity. "I'm sorry," she whispered.

"So am I," Genevieve said with a sigh.

Nearly all of the chairs at the table were filled, and it looked like almost everyone had assembled except for Richard and his parents. Violet was mesmerized by the high ceilings, the length of the table—which would take a good while to walk—and all of the ornate clothing. Even the lower-ranking servants wore finer clothes than Violet had ever owned.

The table was set with bunches of brightly colored flowers, gold and silver plates, and food she didn't recognize laid out in large bowls and platters. None of Violet's dining companions seemed the least amazed or impressed by the setting or the food. She swallowed hard, reminded once more of what an interloper she was in Richard's world.

Suddenly there was a collective intake of breath from the guests seated around the table. Violet turned to see what everyone was looking at in the doorway.

A young woman seemed to float into the room. She had raven black hair and eyes to match. Her skin was so pale Violet had to wonder if she'd ever seen the sun. Her face was proud and her posture rigid. Her magnificent golden dress put all the others, including Violet's, to shame. She was the most beautiful woman Violet had ever seen. Several of the other princesses groaned quietly in dismay.

"Who is that?" Violet asked Genevieve.

"Celeste, the princess of Lore. Everyone thinks she's the one to beat."

"Just because she is pretty? The challenges haven't even begun," Violet said.

A girl to Genevieve's left shook her head. "Don't worry. Celeste is sure to win every one of them. When Celeste wants something, she gets it."

Violet gritted her teeth. Why was it that the daughter of the devious Lore devils who had caused such turmoil and despair during the Great War looked like an angel? Violet had an abrupt desire to tear the other girl apart with her bare hands. Celeste's parents had murdered the royal family—*my family*, Violet reminded herself. She half rose from her chair, her hands clenched, before forcing herself to sit back down. By anyone's measure engaging in a brawl during dinner at the castle was neither ladylike nor sensitive.

Celeste found her seat at the other end of the table. "Are you okay?" Genevieve asked.

"I will be," Violet said, forcing a smile.

The steward clapped his hands twice to get everyone's attention. "Majesties, Highnesses, lords and ladies, I give you King Charles, Queen Martha, and Prince Richard."

Everyone rose to their feet as the royal family entered the banquet hall, and Violet followed suit. Richard walked beside his mother. Watching him at a distance, Violet was struck again by how handsome he was. He also seemed so different in this regal setting, as if he were far away in another world. And for an instant she forgot that he was her Richard, the Richard she had nursed back to health, the Richard she had shared a stolen moment with just minutes before, the Richard who had been leaning in to kiss her, again.

Once Richard and his parents were seated at the head of the table, the rest of the guests seated themselves. Then platters laden with the most exotic food Violet had ever seen, steaming and aromatic, were carried in. The food Violet had assumed was the main course had been only the cold dishes. As she stared at what was set before her, she realized that she was ill prepared to act like a princess, especially since she didn't even know how to eat like one.

There was a bowl of what looked to be clear broth set before each girl. Violet started to pick it up in her hands and then paused. Discreetly, she watched Genevieve to see how she would drink it.

Genevieve reached toward the bowl and put her hands in it. She rinsed them thoroughly before drying them on a cloth set beside her plate. Violet felt herself flushing with embarrassment. She had been about to drink the wash water.

As the dinner progressed, Violet could hear the happy exclamations of the others as they tried first one dish and then another. All of the food must have been delicious, but Violet was so preoccupied with trying to eat like a lady that she barely tasted a thing.

She took a bite of beef and nearly choked.

"Are you okay?" Genevieve asked.

Violet nodded and then quietly asked, "What is this?"

"Beef."

"I know, but what's on it?"

"I don't know which spices," Genevieve confessed, "but they are amazing. If this dinner is a sampling of what the cook can prepare, that alone would make moving here worthwhile."

Violet glanced toward the head of the table and caught Richard staring at her. She flushed and tried to smile. He raised an eyebrow and she smiled wider, hoping to convince him, and herself, that everything was just fine.

Finally, to Violet's relief, there was a lull between

dishes, and the king stood up to address his guests.

"Welcome one and all to Cambria," he began. "We have called you here because it is time for our son Richard to take a wife. With so many beautiful and worthy princesses we realized that choosing one over the other would be impossible. Therefore we devised this contest. The lady who can pass each challenge will demonstrate herself to be the most delicate, the most refined princess of all and will become our son's wife, the princess of Cambria."

There were many murmurs of approval from around the table. But Violet noticed Richard looked as troubled by the situation as when they had spoken of it on the farm.

King Charles continued, "The first test is tomorrow. Ladies, I would suggest you adjourn to your rooms immediately after dinner so that you may be well rested. I want to take this opportunity to wish you all luck. May the most sensitive princess win!"

Violet sat in silence, a feeling of unease growing within her. Meanwhile the girls around her chattered excitedly. Genevieve gave her a cheerful smile, and Violet was hard pressed to return it.

More food continued to arrive from the kitchen, but Violet's stomach was clenched too tightly for her to think about eating any more. She glanced up and down the table, wondering if it would be rude to go to her room.

Did she need to ask the king's permission to leave? Was she expected to stay until dismissed? Inwardly,

Violet groaned in frustration. There were so many things she didn't know. Her parents had raised her to be honest and hardworking. They knew nothing of courts and kings and etiquette and could never have prepared her for her current situation.

"Is something wrong?" Genevieve asked.

"I don't feel well," Violet admitted. She didn't like sharing her discomfort, but she realized Genevieve was the only one who might help her get the answers she needed.

"Are you sick?" Genevieve asked, leaning away in alarm.

Violet shook her head. "No, just exhausted. I would like to lie down and get some rest."

Genevieve signaled to a servant, who approached. "Could you tell the king that my companion and I are tired and wish to retire for the evening?" Genevieve asked sweetly.

The man bowed and then hurried to the head of the table, where he spoke to the king. King Charles looked down the table at Genevieve and Violet, smiled at them, and nodded.

"Let's go," Genevieve said, rising.

"You don't have to leave if you don't want to," Violet protested.

"Nonsense, I couldn't eat another bite. Besides, you heard what King Charles said about getting our rest. I have a feeling we're going to need it."

As Violet followed Genevieve from the hall, she resolved to watch and copy the other girl's mannerisms and behavior, since she hadn't the slightest inkling of how she was supposed to act.

Approaching the staircase, Violet began to look around her. When she had first arrived, her thoughts had been consumed with her task, and she hadn't taken a close look at her surroundings. Without guests streaming down it, the empty staircase was wide enough that Violet could lie down flat on a stair and still leave enough room for people to walk up on either side of her. The dark wood seemed to glow in the light from all the candles and torches that adorned it.

At the top of the staircase Violet saw three long corridors, in addition to the one that led to her room, dimly lit by candlelight. She stood for a moment, peering down each of them and breathlessly wondering which one led to Richard's bedroom.

Genevieve cleared her throat to politely get Violet's attention and started walking toward their room. Violet dropped her eyes to the stone floor and hurried down the hall after her.

Back in their room Genevieve collapsed in the chair she had been sitting in earlier. "So what did you think of our competition?" she asked.

Violet immediately thought of Celeste, and she felt anger rushing through her. It wasn't right that she was there competing. Competing as if nothing had happened, as if her family hadn't slaughtered Cambria's royal family. *No, not just the royal family,* Violet reminded herself. *My family.*

"Is something wrong?" Genevieve asked, concerned.

Violet shook her head and glanced down at her hands. Her fists were clenched so tightly that her fingernails were cutting into her palms. She forced her muscles to relax, and she did her best to put Celeste from her thoughts. After all, it was the girl's parents who were to blame for the past, not the girl herself.

Violet took a deep breath and thought about the other princesses she had met at the table. "They all looked very beautiful and seemed quite pleasant."

Genevieve stared at her for a moment and then giggled. "They're princesses. Of course they were."

"So, I guess all princesses are beautiful?"

Genevieve giggled harder. "No."

Violet stared at her, confused. "But you just said—"

"You commented that they all *looked* beautiful. That's true, but it doesn't mean they are. With skilled help even the plainest person can be beautiful."

"Really?" Violet asked, her eyes widening at the thought.

"Really. Although, clearly, that's something you've never had to worry about."

"Where I come from, how I looked was not important," Violet said.

"We should all be so lucky," Genevieve said.

"I think you're teasing," Violet said.

Genevieve shook her head. "Do you remember the girl sitting across from you?"

"Yes?"

"She had a wart on her chin."

"No!"

"Yes. And the girl across from me—"

"You mean the one with the brilliant white teeth?"

"I mean the one with the brilliant fake white teeth."

Violet gasped.

"The girl with the red hair that was so perfect it almost didn't seem real—wig."

Violet sat down on her bed and began to laugh until tears streamed down her face. It felt good to laugh. There had been so much darkness, so much sorrow lately, that finding something to laugh about was a relief. "Okay, what about Celeste? What's she hiding?" Violet finally gasped.

Genevieve's smile faded. "A cold, mean heart."

Violet stopped laughing. "Are you sure?"

"Yes. I can read people. It is something of a gift. Her physical beauty is genuine enough, but her spirit is another matter."

Violet shuddered. Celeste was the daughter of people who had had an entire family killed in their sleep. To expect her to be a warm, caring person would be to expect an apple tree to produce oranges.

"We probably should get some sleep," Genevieve said.

"Yes," Violet said, realizing for the first time how exhausted she was.

She turned to look at her bed and wondered for

a moment if she would even be able to sleep in it. It was incredibly soft, much more so than what she was used to. It stood several inches higher from the ground than hers as well and was piled with furs and blankets.

Undressing quickly, Violet slipped between the sheets. It was softer than lying in a field of spring grass. She thought about Richard sleeping in her tiny, hard bed at home and marveled that he had been able to get any rest.

In the quiet of the dark room Violet's thoughts turned to home, and she found it hard to believe that she had left there only hours before. Outside, the storm still lashed against the castle, the rain drumming on the windowpanes. Violet wondered how her mother was feeling and felt tears slip out from under her closed eyelids.

An hour later Violet was still awake, wishing she could fall asleep. Sorrow for her mother had been replaced with a feeling of restlessness in her strange surroundings. Violet could hear Genevieve snoring, and she had to bite her lip to keep from laughing. If the king or queen happened to walk by the room, Genevieve would find herself disqualified before the competition had even begun.

But Violet stopped grinning when she heard the sound of soft footfalls. She held her breath, wondering for one wild moment if King Charles and Queen Martha were really checking to see who might be snoring in their sleep. Her trepidation gave way to curiosity as she realized that it didn't sound like the shuffling of a human's step.

A wet nose touched her hand. Violet sat up with a start and saw Richard's dog standing next to her bed. He held something in his mouth. She stretched out her hand and he dropped a roll of parchment into it. "Good, Duke," Violet whispered, scratching him behind his ears.

Duke leaned into her hand for a moment. Then he turned and left the room. Genevieve was still snoring, so Violet decided to risk lighting the candle on the table by her bed. The flame flared brightly to life, and she shielded it with her hand as she glanced toward the other girl's bed. Genevieve continued to snore.

Violet carefully unrolled the parchment. The letter had been written in a strong, sure hand. *Violet, if you hope to pass the test tomorrow, do as I instruct.* Richard had done as he promised. Violet breathed a sigh of relief before reading on.

CHAPTER SIX

Richard couldn't sleep, and dawn found him pacing in front of his parents' chambers. At last his mother opened the door, saw him standing there, and held it wide for him to enter. His father was also up and sitting at a table, quill in hand. Prince Richard walked in, closed the door, and said, "If Violet is the true princess of Cambria, then she should be restored to the throne."

His parents both winced, but he could tell they had expected him to say it.

"If she is the true princess of Cambria, then she should be," Queen Martha agreed. "However, there's no way to be certain."

"What about the nurse who took her from the castle?"

"No such person has come forth in the last seventeen years. If there was a nurse, she is probably long since dead," Richard's father said.

Richard crossed his arms over his chest and stood, feet planted. "Is it even possible that her story is true? I always thought the infant princess died."

His parents exchanged a glance and then Richard's mother nodded. "It might be true; the girl's body was never found."

Richard stared at them in shock. "Why didn't you tell me?"

His father sighed. "Son, you have to understand. When the royal family was murdered, Cambria trembled on the brink of conquest and utter ruin. We were nearly killed by another noble family amid the turmoil. When your mother and I ascended to the throne and led Cambria to victory over Lore, we pledged to keep the missing princess a secret. If everyone knew, then any number of pretenders would have been presented at court, and the kingdom could have once again been thrust into chaos—and possibly even civil war. We reasoned that if someone had hidden the princess, sooner or later they would have revealed themselves."

"But no nurse has come forward. So, why do you hesitate to believe that Violet is the princess?"

"We had reason to believe that the baby was either drowned in the river by the Lore assassins or abducted by them," he said.

"If she was abducted by them, then that would mean—"

"That she was raised in Lore," his mother said. "That Celeste could be the true princess of Cambria."

Richard felt his blood run cold, and he shook his head. "That's unthinkable."

"I wish it were," his mother said grimly. "There's a very real possibility that if she does not win this contest, the king and queen of Lore will try to claim that the Cambrian throne is hers anyway."

"Why not strike first and declare Violet the real princess of Cambria?" Richard asked.

"We must continue with this contest or risk offending eighteen other kingdoms. If your Violet is everything you believe her to be, she will be the winner, and we can then use her existence to counter any claim presented by Lore."

"And what if neither Violet nor Celeste wins?" Richard asked.

"Then you shall marry the winner immediately, and her parents will support us in whatever comes," his father said.

Prince Richard shook his head. "It's always about politics," he said.

"Always. And as prince you would do well to remember that," his father said.

"But I love Violet."

"It's a noble sentiment, but treaties and alliances are based on mutual self-interest and gain, not love," King Charles said.

"All is not lost," the queen added. "She may win."

"How?" Richard asked bitterly. "These contests you have arranged are absurd. I very much doubt that most noblewomen could pass them, let alone Violet, who has worked her entire life and known nothing of ease or finery."

"You must have more faith in her, and in us," Queen Martha said.

Richard paused and stared at her for a moment, trying to interpret her meaning. "Is there something you haven't told me?" he asked at last.

"We have told you everything you need to know," his father said.

But not everything I want to know, he thought. Richard debated whether or not to press the issue further but sensed he would get nothing more from his parents at the moment. But Richard could play that game too. He didn't know all that his parents were planning, but he could do everything in his power to make sure that at the end it was Violet and not Celeste who was still standing.

Violet woke up and lay still, taking in her environment. So much had happened in the last twenty-four hours she could scarcely believe it. She thought of her parents and wished that they might be well and happy. She sat up slowly. The bed was so soft it was hard to get out of it.

She glanced across the room and saw Genevieve also beginning to wake. Violet struggled out of bed and retrieved her gown from the night before. It seemed too fancy to wear during the day, but her own clothes were ruined from her journey and seemed to have disappeared from the room as well.

Violet dressed quickly in her green gown and then sat to brush her hair. The snarls and the tangles were nearly too much for the brush, and she winced in pain as it pulled at her hair. She heard Genevieve get up and move around, but Violet was focused on the task at hand.

"Would you like me to brush it for you?" Genevieve asked suddenly.

Violet jumped to see Genevieve standing an arm's length away. "No, I'm fine," Violet said quickly.

Genevieve shrugged and went back to her side of the room. *I should just tell her so she'll understand*, Violet thought. She bit her tongue, though, and continued to battle her tangled blond locks. A couple of minutes later Genevieve's maids bustled in and began to fuss over Genevieve.

"I'm going to breakfast," Violet said, having arranged her hair as best she could.

"I'll be there shortly," Genevieve assured her through gritted teeth.

Downstairs Violet walked from room to room, taking in the immensity of the castle. She walked by the throne room, but it was empty. She kept walking, watching as servants went through their morning routines.

Suddenly she heard what sounded like Richard's voice as she approached another room. She paused for a moment, not wanting to interrupt. ". . . wish you luck in the competition," he was saying.

"I won't need it," a sultry voice purred.

Violet's heart began to pound. She started to move away, not wanting to be caught eavesdropping. Not a moment later Celeste appeared in the hallway, looking even more beautiful than she had the night before at dinner. A smug smile was firmly in place, and it didn't falter even a bit when she saw Violet.

"Oh, you. Girl, can you fetch me some water?"

"Excuse me?" Violet asked, when she realized Celeste was talking to her.

"Oh, sorry, I thought you were one of the servants," Celeste said.

"I'm not," Violet said haughtily.

"Are you sure about that?" Celeste asked bluntly. "Listen, you might as well go home; I've got this competition as good as won."

"If you don't mind, I think I'll stay," Violet said through gritted teeth.

Celeste shrugged. "Whatever. You probably won't even make it past the first test. I mean, look at you. Those rough hands; the way you walk. I even thought you were going to drink the wash water yesterday. It's obvious you're not sensitive. It's also obvious that you're a fake."

Violet opened her mouth to protest but could think of nothing to say. Celeste was right, and from the look on her face she knew it. Celeste continued on her way, smirking.

Violet thought about going back to her room, but she wasn't ready to face cheerful conversation with Genevieve. Instead Violet made her way to the great hall. She discovered that she was the first to arrive and took her seat from the night before. Harried-looking servants passed to and fro with barely a glance in her direction.

One woman entered the room, saw Violet, and made straight for her. Violet recognized her as the woman who had brought her the beautiful dress. The woman looked agitated, and she was wringing her hands.

"Begging your pardon, my lady."

"What is it?" Violet asked, a note of concern in her voice. Violet feared that the king and queen had rethought their decision to allow her to compete and had sent this woman to deliver the news.

"I'm sorry. I just now put the rest of your things in your room."

"My things?"

"Your other clothes and such. I was meant to do it last night."

"What is your name?" Violet asked.

"Mary, my lady."

"Mary, who gave you this dress to give to me?" Violet asked eagerly.

Mary just looked at her, confused. "Why, no one, my lady. I was told by the steward that it was your dress and to take it up to you along with the rest of your things."

"Oh, well, thank you," Violet said.

Mary nodded and then scurried away. Violet was no closer to discovering her benefactor's identity.

Genevieve arrived at the table a few minutes later.

"The rest of your things were delivered to the room," she said cheerfully.

"So I heard."

Not long after, everyone else was seated around the table, including Richard and his parents. Compared to dinner the night before, everyone ate breakfast in relative silence. Violet guessed she wasn't the only one who was nervous. The rich food wasn't helping her to calm down either. As breakfast came to a close, the king stood up to make an announcement.

"As you know, the competition begins today. The first challenge tests your sensitivity. There will be four pairs of threads set before you. In each pair one thread is silk and one is cotton. You must choose the silk thread in each pair. Those who correctly identify all four silk threads may remain. The rest may leave or stay as they wish, but they will not continue to the next challenge."

All around Violet heads nodded in understanding of the challenge. Violet's heart sank. Were these girls' hands really so delicate, so sensitive, that they could tell silk from cotton in a single thread?

"You may return to your rooms. The steward will come for each of you one at a time."

Back in their room Violet could not sit still, and she paced the floor. *Left, left, right, left.* That was what Richard had written to her. That was how she should choose.

"At least this first challenge should be easy," Genevieve said, attempting to make conversation as she sat at the table and watched Violet.

It took all of Violet's willpower to keep from laughing. She had never even touched a silk garment. "So, all princesses should be able to tell the difference?" Violet asked.

Genevieve shrugged. "Any who have done embroidery, which would be most." She sighed. "It's one of the few activities I'm ever allowed to do."

"I've never done any embroidery," Violet admitted.

Genevieve's eyes widened. "Do they keep you locked in a tower?"

"No."

"Have you been asleep for several years after being cursed?"

"No."

"Then how come?"

"I did . . . other things."

"Like what?"

"I can cook. I make a great berry pie," Violet said. "I was planning on entering one in the contest at the festival."

Genevieve stared at Violet, mouth gaping. "They let you in the kitchen?" she squealed at last.

"Of course."

"And they weren't afraid you would burn yourself or cut yourself?"

Violet laughed. "Of course not. I learned how to

handle knives and how to treat fire with respect when I was little."

A sudden knock came at the door. The steward appeared. "Princess Violet, the king and queen are ready for you," he said.

Her heart in her throat Violet followed the steward to the throne room. There were fewer people there this time, just the king, the queen, a few servants, and a handful of petitioners. Violet looked around for Richard but was disappointed to discover he was absent.

"Approach, Princess," the king said.

Violet couldn't help but wonder if he called all of the princesses by their title because he couldn't remember their names—or just her. She stepped forward, and there on a table were the four sets of threads. *Left, left, right, left.* That's what the parchment had said. Violet prayed Richard had gotten it right.

"Tell us, which of the threads are silk?" the queen asked.

Violet touched each one in turn, closing her eyes as she did so she could concentrate on her sense of touch. In dismay she realized that she truly couldn't tell the difference between any of the threads. After touching the last thread, Violet opened her eyes and looked at Richard's parents, who were leaning forward on their thrones, awaiting her answer.

"The silk ones are here on the left, here on the

left, there on the right, and here on the left," she said, indicating each in turn.

Violet looked up and held her breath, waiting for their pronouncement. "Thank you," the king said. He waved his hand and then turned aside to talk with the steward.

Violet stood for a moment and then realized that she had been dismissed. "Excuse me, Your Majesty?"

The king looked back at Violet, clearly startled at the interruption. She could tell she had made some sort of mistake, but since the damage was done, she pressed on. "Did I pass the test?"

"We will make an announcement this evening at dinner," he said. "You may go for now."

Violet had just reached the door when she heard the king say, "Just a minute. Violet?"

Violet turned in dismay. Being demoted from "Princess" to just "Violet" couldn't be a good thing.

"Yes, Your Majesty?"

"I would like you to stay for a minute. Come here, please."

Violet hurried to stand before the thrones again. "We're hearing petitions today. Competition or no, work still continues."

She didn't know what to say, so she just remained quiet.

"Two men are disputing over the right to farm a piece of land. I believe it is near your father's. I'm going to let them argue their cases, and if I have any questions, I would like you to answer them. I would like to have an unbiased answer from someone who might be in a position to know a thing or two about farming."

"I'd be happy to assist in any way I can," Violet said, and curtsied.

"Steward, bring them in," the king instructed.

Two farmers entered and came before the king. One was tall, with eyes like a hawk, and the other was short, with ruddy cheeks.

"Please share your complaint."

The ruddy-faced one spoke up. "Sire, the land that I farm requires water for irrigation, which comes from a stream. We are neighbors and have always had an agreement to share the water. Two weeks ago, though, he dammed the water on his land, and now my crops are dying."

"We had no such agreement regarding the water," the tall one insisted.

"Steward, how many bushels does each produce a year from the land he works?" the king asked.

Violet listened as the steward gave his answer. She studied the two men closely. The argument was over whether or not there had been an agreement, which meant one of them was lying. The question was, which one?

Each man continued to argue his side, while the king asked additional questions. Violet watched each man closely as he responded, and even more closely when he was listening to the other one.

"Violet, what do you think?" the king asked quietly.

She was surprised that the king would ask her opinion. "The tall man is lying."

"Are you sure?"

"Yes." She nodded, convinced finally of the truth. "They had an agreement; the tall one is lying."

"How do you know that?"

"Given the crops being raised, the short man could not possibly expect to plant and harvest without a steady supply of water. He would have been a fool not to have an agreement with his neighbor."

"And what makes you think he's not a fool?"

Violet answered, "Because he looks you in the eyes; he's hiding nothing. The tall one won't look anyone here in the eyes, including his neighbor."

"Thank you, Violet. I appreciate your insight," the king said. "Steward, make sure the dam is removed from the stream."

The steward bowed and escorted the two men out. "Violet, you may leave now," the king said.

"Thank you," she answered, not sure what else to say, and left.

Violet returned to her room, where Genevieve was waiting, wide-eyed. "You were gone for so long!"

"There was a lot going on down there," Violet said.

"Did you pass?"

"I don't know. They are going to announce the results at dinner."

"That's cruel! Waiting the whole day is going to be dreadful."

"Princess Genevieve, Their Majesties are ready for you," said the steward from the doorway.

Genevieve stood up from her chair and followed him out. Violet wanted to wish her good luck, but in truth she hoped that every other girl failed, including Genevieve.

Violet sat down in a chair and stared at the window looking toward her village in the distance. She tried not to think about the test, or Richard, or her mother. It left her very little to think about.

CHAPTER SEVEN

Genevieve was subdued when she returned from the test.

"How did you do?" Violet asked.

"Fine. I could tell which threads were silk."

Violet's heart fell, but she struggled to smile. "Then why aren't you happy and smiling?"

"Someday I'll be queen of my own country or another. There are some things I'm not looking forward to in that regard. I complain that I never get to do anything, which is true. Some of the responsibilities of being queen, though, I don't want."

"I'm sorry."

Genevieve shrugged. "Let's talk about something happy."

"Like what?"

"Like how we're going to fix your hair for dinner tonight."

Violet laughed. "That's not exactly what comes to my mind when I think of happy."

Genevieve grinned from ear to ear. "Are you kidding? This could be great. No one ever lets me fix my own hair, so I can at least do yours."

Violet couldn't help but smile at Genevieve's enthusiasm. An hour later the smile had turned into a grimace as Genevieve put the finishing touches on her hair. "Ouch," Violet said.

"Sorry. Your hair was really tangled," Genevieve said. "Not anymore, though. I think you'll like it."

She handed Violet a looking glass. "It's amazing," Violet said in awe. Half her hair was piled high atop her head, and the rest of it cascaded down in waves.

"I'm glad you like it," Genevieve said, pride in her voice.

There was a knock at the door, and once again the steward appeared. "Ladies, there will be a ball tonight following dinner."

Genevieve squealed in excitement, and the man backed out of the room.

"Perfect, your hair is already done."

"Do you want me to hold your maids at bay so you can fix your own?" Violet asked, standing up to stretch her legs.

"Could you? That would be wonderful!"

Violet reached the doorway just in time to intercept the maids. "Her Highness does not require your services," Violet told them.

"We're here to take care of her and to make sure

she shines," the one in charge said, her jaw set stubbornly.

Violet smiled serenely and straightened her posture. She was at least three inches taller, and she took advantage of the height difference. "The princess needs no help shining. When she has need of your services, she will call for you."

The maid looked like she was about to argue with her. "Please make them go away," she heard Genevieve whisper.

Violet took a deep breath. "You will go now or suffer my wrath." She put as much authority into her voice as possible. She was a princess, and even if she wasn't, they didn't know that. The maids might be used to pushing Genevieve around, confident that they had her parents' backing. But if they were smart, they would know better than to defy a princess they were not responsible for readying.

It worked. Grudgingly, all three women dropped their eyes and took several steps back. "She will send for you when she has need of you," Violet said. "You may go now."

The three maids turned and walked down the hall. Violet watched them until they were out of sight and then sagged against the door frame.

"You were magnificent!" Genevieve said. "Thank you ever so much."

"You're welcome. If you don't look your best tonight, though, I'm sure the tall one is going to have my head."

While Genevieve began to work on her hair, Violet investigated the armoire which held the clothes that had been sent for her. There were half a dozen dresses ranging from a simple blue dress to a stunning black one that looked fit for a queen.

"Do we wear different dresses to the ball than to dinner?" Violet asked.

"That depends entirely on our choosing. Most of the girls will probably change between dinner and the ball. I would just as soon only have to change once."

"Me too."

"So let's wear the dresses we want to wear to the ball and pledge to each other that we won't spill food on them."

"Done," Violet said with a smile. "I think I've found the perfect dress." She pulled out a lavender gown that was the same color as her eyes.

"Perfect," the other girl breathed.

Violet picked at her food, too nervous to eat. She noticed that around her most of the others were doing the same. Genevieve and a girl with silvery white hair seemed to be the only ones with an appetite.

Violet kept stealing glances at Richard. He didn't seem to be eating either and seemed uncomfortable. Was it possible that even he didn't know the results? Or did he perhaps know that she had failed?

At last the king called them all to attention. Violet could feel fear and excitement filling the room.

"As you know, the first test was given today. Seventeen of you passed."

Violet's jaw dropped. Genevieve was right. The princesses who embroidered could tell the difference, whereas her work-hardened hands could not. In dismay she wondered about the three who had failed and was sure that she was one of them.

"Julianna, Rowena, and Esther, you are free to go, or to stay, if you like, to enjoy the festivities."

The three young women rose from the table, curtsied, and left the room.

Violet sat very still. She had passed the first test, and she was still in the competition! Part of her, though, felt horrible that she had only passed because Richard and Duke had helped her. But if she had been raised as a princess, she would probably have been able to tell the difference.

"Congratulations," Genevieve whispered.

"Thanks. You too."

Violet glanced up to the head of the table and saw Richard smiling at her, a look of relief on his face. So he hadn't known in advance who had passed either.

Violet surveyed the rest of the competition. Relief and excitement were the predominating emotions on people's faces. Everyone who had been too nervous to touch her food at dinner now ate the dessert set before her voraciously.

Dinner came to a close, and all of the guests left the table, having been informed that the ball would commence in an hour. Most of the girls headed for their rooms. Violet and Genevieve decided to pass the time outside instead. The night was serene, the sky was clear, and thousands of stars shone brightly.

They strolled through the garden. Even though it was nighttime, many torches were lit along the pathway, and Violet marveled at everything around her. There were statues that towered over her, fountains that fed tiny ponds, and an endless variety of flowers. Everything was beautiful, and it took Violet's breath away. Genevieve noticed.

"You act like you've never seen a garden before."

"I've seen plenty of fields of wildflowers and crops, but none that were for decoration instead of food."

Genevieve gave her a strange look, but before she could say anything, they spied a girl sitting alone on one of the benches. She had golden hair that fell in rings to her shoulders. She was weeping.

"Who is that?" Violet asked in a whisper. She knew it wasn't one of the three girls who had failed the test.

"That's Goldie. I feel sorry for her."

"Why?" Violet asked.

"Her parents died a couple of years ago. She's set to become queen when she turns eighteen. Her uncle is currently acting as regent."

"What's wrong with that?"

"I don't trust him. He's a foul man, and I would be surprised if she lives to see that birthday."

"That's terrible!" Violet gasped, her heart going out to the other girl.

"I think she suspects so too. That's one of the

reasons she's so eager to marry Prince Richard. Her uncle wouldn't dare try anything then."

"But wouldn't she and Richard rule both kingdoms then?" Violet asked.

Genevieve shrugged. "They'd rule hers until his parents die. Then, who knows? Maybe a lost heir of Cambria will appear. You know, there have been rumors that a baby escaped the massacre here."

"So I've heard," Violet said, hastily averting her eyes.

"You know, you've never said which kingdom you're from," Genevieve said suddenly.

"From this one," Violet said, taking a deep breath.

Genevieve put a hand on Violet's arm, and Violet turned to face her.

"You? You're the lost heir of Cambria?"

"I don't know what I am," Violet confessed. "Until two days ago I was just a farm girl. Then my parents told me that a woman had entrusted me to their safekeeping when I was an infant and that they thought that I could be the princess."

"This is incredible!" Genevieve said, pulling her away from Goldie for a little privacy. "This means that you are the rightful queen of Cambria."

Violet shook her head. "That's not what I want."

"Then what do you want?"

"Richard," she said with a sigh.

"That I can't help you with," Genevieve said.

Violet looked over her shoulder. "Do you think we should go talk to Goldie?"

Genevieve shook her head. "I think she wants to be alone."

"Maybe that's just because she feels alone."

Genevieve sighed. "You have a point."

Together they retraced their steps and approached Goldie. The other girl looked up, startled, at their approach.

Violet and Genevieve sat down on either side of her. "Is there something wrong?" Violet asked.

Goldie nodded. "You've seen my tears. It's no use lying about them."

"Is there anything we can do to help?" Violet asked.

"Yes."

Violet was surprised, but she reached out and took Goldie's hand. "What is it?"

"Promise me that if one of you wins this challenge, you will help me in my coming struggle with my uncle."

"I do not know how I can help, but I will certainly try," Violet promised.

"As will I," Genevieve said.

"Thank you," Goldie said, squeezing Violet's hand, then stood abruptly and wiped away her tears. "Come now. We have a ball to attend."

The three walked along the garden pathway toward the castle. Violet heard a noise behind her and turned in time to glimpse a woman disappearing around a hedge. Violet thought she might follow the woman to see who it was, but she decided against it. She had not said anything of which she was ashamed.

Inside the castle the table in the great hall had been cleared away to make room for dancing, and several musicians were tuning their instruments. A number of young noblemen gathered in the elegant space, and Violet was relieved. She had envisioned each princess trying to dance with Richard while everyone else just stood and watched. With more people dancing, Violet hoped she would be able to disguise the fact that she couldn't dance.

None of the other princesses were present yet, and the steward bustled up to the three of them and directed them to wait in another room.

As Violet took a seat in the drawing room as the steward had instructed, she asked the other girls, "Why do we have to wait here?"

"So that they can properly introduce us," Goldie said.

A few minutes later more of the competitors joined them. They sat and talked together, laughing and comparing stories about their home lives. It was fascinating to listen to, and Violet felt even more that theirs were lives she would never understand. They all seemed to sparkle in ball gowns, each more spectacular than the next. Celeste was the last to arrive, and her black dress, which was shot through with silver threads, was breathtaking.

At last the steward returned, and all seventeen of them followed him to the entrance of the ballroom.

Violet strained to see into the room. And when she finally glimpsed Richard, wearing his crown, his blue tunic emblazoned with gold, her heart skipped a beat.

"Majesties, ladies and gentlemen, I would like to present the princesses," the steward announced.

The room quieted, and all eyes turned toward them. "Princess Celeste of Lore," he said in a booming, authoritative voice, and Celeste sailed into the room, curtsied, and then walked slowly down the length of the room before turning at the end.

He called nine other girls Violet didn't know, who mimicked what Celeste had done.

"Princess Genevieve of Antiqua."

Genevieve walked in, curtsied, and joined the others at the far end.

"Princess Goldie of Northland."

Goldie floated into the room and Violet marveled at her poise. If she hadn't seen it with her own eyes, she would never have believed the princess had been sobbing just a few minutes before.

One by one the others entered, until only Violet was left waiting in the drawing room. She stepped forward, and the steward announced, "Princess Violet."

Violet did her best to curtsy gracefully and glide to the far end of the room without tripping over herself. She noted the omission of a kingdom following her name, and she knew the others had too. The question of her lineage hung in the air around her and made her uncomfortable. Still, she couldn't have expected the steward would announce her as Princess Violet of Cambria. She knew she should just be grateful he had called her a princess at all.

A moment later the king and queen moved toward the center of the room. They were magnificent together, moving with a grace and ease that Violet could never hope to achieve. The musicians began to play. King Charles and Queen Martha danced, spinning together around and around on the floor until Violet felt dizzy just watching them.

The dance ended, and then the king and queen invited others to join them as the music started for a new dance. Violet took a step back toward the wall as a wave of young men descended upon the group of princesses.

"What's wrong?" Genevieve asked.

"I don't know how to dance," Violet said.

"That's okay; neither do I," a smiling man said, offering her his hand. "I am Roland, count of Argess."

"Violet," she responded. She took his hand, and he led her onto the dance floor. She lost track of how many times she stepped on his foot, but she was quick to notice that he was very kind and a much better dancer than he had let on. He just kept smiling and talking, never starting or making a comment that she was tripping all over him.

The next two men Violet danced with weren't as gracious, grimacing every time she stepped on one of their feet, but they didn't say a word about it either.

"You are going to leave some of them intact for

the rest of us, aren't you?" Genevieve joked as they both sat out a dance.

"I don't know. Depends on whether or not they get the warning and stay away."

"Just do us all a favor and wait to dance with Richard until the rest of us have had a turn," Genevieve said.

Violet looked at her suspiciously, and Genevieve just shrugged. "It isn't every day a girl gets to dance with a prince, even if she is a princess."

"Who is that girl?" Violet asked, pointing to the one dancing with Richard. She had skin so pale it almost seemed to glow, and her lovely face was crowned by silver white hair.

"That's Arianna; she's from Aster. They say her mother is a mermaid," Genevieve added conspiratorially.

Violet couldn't help but laugh. "A mermaid, really?"

"That's what I've heard," Genevieve said. "I can't tell you if it's true or not. That's not even the strangest part."

"Okay, what?" Violet asked.

"I hear Arianna's in love with a prince who's descended from werewolves."

"You're making that up!" Violet accused.

"No, I swear it's true. Or at least that's what I've heard."

"If she's in love with another man, then why is she here?" Violet asked, choosing for the moment not to dwell on the werewolf part.

"What are any of us doing here?" Genevieve asked. "Maybe her parents forced her to join the competition to strengthen her kingdom's alliances, or maybe Arianna is trying to make her werewolf jealous."

"Isn't anyone here for love?" Violet said under her breath.

"Only you."

Violet startled. "How do you know that?"

Genevieve rolled her eyes. "Please, it is so obvious. Everyone knows you love him."

"Then why don't they all leave?" she asked bitterly.

Genevieve patted Violet on the shoulder. "Like I said, some of us aren't here by choice. Even still, though, Richard is an excellent catch. He's strong, kind, and handsome. Don't get me wrong, I don't love him, but I'm sure I could learn to love him. Anyone could. Now smile—your prince is headed this way."

As Prince Richard approached, he held out his hand to Violet. She took it and followed him onto the dance floor. "I don't know how to dance," she admitted.

"That's okay—just move with me," he said, one hand holding hers and the other on her waist.

She looked down at his feet. "No," he said.

She looked up at him. "What?"

"Don't look at our feet; look right here, in my eyes," he said.

"But how will I know which way to move?" she protested.

Richard's hand tightened around her waist, and his fingers pressed into her back until she stepped closer to him. "You'll just know," he whispered into her ear.

Violet gazed deep into his eyes, and when he began to move, she moved with him. She didn't know if it was the subtle pressure changes in his fingers, or the movements of his eyes, but somehow Violet knew just which way to move while she was dancing with Richard. They started slowly and then began to pick up speed until they were twirling around the room.

Violet kept her eyes locked on Richard's, afraid that if she looked away, the moment would end, and the magic would be lost.

"You have bewitched me," he whispered.

She shook her head. "I'm afraid I'm the one under your spell."

"Then I hope it lasts forever," he said.

"Forever," she breathed.

The music stopped, and after a moment so did they. "I'll send Duke to visit you again once I know what the next challenge is," he leaned close to murmur.

"I wish you would send yourself instead," she breathed.

"One day I just might."

CHAPTER EIGHT

"You can't be serious," Richard said, staring at his mother.

"Quite serious," she replied.

"The next test is to see who feels intense pain over the loss of a single pulled hair?"

"Yes, that's it exactly," she said.

Richard sat down and passed a hand over his weary face. He was still wearing his finery from the ball, and his feet were sore from having danced continuously for hours. He just wanted to send a message to Violet and then get some sleep. "Seriously, what are you and Father doing?" he asked.

"Exactly what we said we would do. We're looking for a young woman of great sensitivity."

"But it's so absurd. I mean, would *you* feel intense pain over the loss of a single hair?"

Queen Martha smiled, but there was a touch of sadness in it. "I always do."

Richard knew, instinctively, that his mother was talking about something else; he just couldn't figure out what it was. He thought about pleading with her again to end the whole contest but knew it would be no use. Richard's mother was the only person in Cambria more stubborn than his father.

"Don't worry. If you're meant to be with her, it will work out that way," she said, softly.

"But why can't I just be with her? Why must there be all of these games?"

His mother didn't answer him, probably because she had nothing new to say on the subject. Frustrated, Richard stood to go. "Sleep well, Mother."

"And you, my son."

Richard left and headed to his room. He lit the candle on his writing desk and took out a parchment. He dipped his quill in the inkwell and began to write.

Dearest. Only five more challenges. Tomorrow's will be simple. All you must do is pretend to be in great pain when a single hair is plucked from your head. It's absurd, I know, but for now we must play along. Yours, Richard.

As soon as the ink had dried, Richard rolled up the parchment and whistled. Duke, who had been sleeping at the foot of his bed, awoke and bounded over to the desk. Richard let the dog sniff the napkin that Violet had used at dinner. "Remember Violet, Duke? Remember going to see her last night?"

Prince Richard held out the parchment, and the dog took it in his mouth. "Okay, boy, go find her!"

The dog trotted out of the room, and Richard put his head down on his desk. What was he, a prisoner? A prisoner who had to send secret messages via a dog? It made him sick, but he saw no other way out.

Violet was waiting for Duke when he arrived. She took the letter from him with trembling hands. She lit the candle on her bedside table and read the letter three times, just to be sure she understood.

To test herself Violet plucked a single hair from her head. She barely felt it. It was more of an annoyance than anything else. Violet sighed deeply. Tomorrow she needed to convince the others, and herself, that it was a lot more than just an annoyance.

"Thank you, Duke," she whispered. She patted the dog on the head and then watched as he left the room.

Violet lay down and tried to sleep, but thoughts of Richard crowded her mind. She thought of the dance they had shared. It had been so perfect. A perfect moment in an otherwise imperfect day.

In the morning Violet woke well before Genevieve. She dressed in silence and made her way downstairs, watching as servants cleaned and carried and made preparations for the day. Violet wanted desperately to help. For the first time in her life she felt useless, and she longed for a physical task that would take her mind off of everything that was happening.

In the great hall the steward approached her. "Princess Violet, a messenger arrived early this morning who wished to speak with you," he said.

Immediately Violet thought of her mother. "Where can I find the messenger?" she asked hurriedly.

"I believe he's in the kitchen. I can summon him for you."

"No, that's okay," Violet said, already headed for the kitchen.

"But my lady—"

Violet just kept walking. When she entered the kitchen, several servants rushed forward, protesting, and she thought about what Genevieve had said about never having been allowed in a kitchen. Violet scanned the room for a familiar face.

"Violet, over here!"

She turned and saw Thomas. The boy hastened up to her and regarded her with awe. "I hardly recognized you," he said.

"Thomas, what news?" Violet asked, too afraid to engage in pleasantries with him.

His brow furrowed. "Your father sent me to tell you that he won't yet be joining you. Your mother's health is doing worse and worse. They send you their love and are remembering you in their prayers."

"She's still alive?" Violet asked, hope touching her suddenly.

Thomas nodded solemnly. "Father Paul doesn't think she's going to make it, though."

"But she's made it this far."

Thomas nodded again.

"Thank you," Violet said. It didn't take away all

the fear or worry, but it was a small relief to know that she was still okay. "Are you going to be staying?" she asked Thomas.

He shook his head. "I'm just getting some breakfast, and then I have to return to the farm. Your father's had to hire my older brothers to help get harvest done in time for the Feasting. He's put me in charge of them," he told her importantly.

Violet smiled. "You make sure and keep them in line."

Thomas nodded. "Don't worry; I'm keeping a good eye on your parents, too. That's why I have to get back, though."

"Would you tell my parents I love them both?"

"I will," he promised.

When Violet returned to the great hall, she felt a little more at ease than she had earlier.

The morning meal was a quiet affair, and she suspected everyone was exhausted from the previous evening's events. The king made no announcement about the day's challenge, but he told everyone that the steward would come get them when it was their turn, as he had the day before.

Upstairs in their room Violet watched as Genevieve did some needlework. The other girl tried to teach her a couple of stitches, but Violet was too distracted to pay very close attention.

Finally, the steward came to their room, but this time he escorted out Genevieve first. Violet had to wait only a few minutes before she returned, rubbing the back of her head absently. Then it was Violet's turn to follow the steward, who led her not to the throne room but to the queen's chambers.

Violet was overwhelmed by the grandeur. The bed was monstrous, the size of her house. Rich red tapestries draped down the walls. A pair of matching chairs invited her to sit with their bright cushions. A writing table stood against one wall. There was another table with a white top ribboned with black streaks that was unlike anything Violet had ever seen. The queen rose when she entered, and Violet fought the urge to drop to her knees before the stately woman.

Violet was offered a chair, and she sat while the queen made small talk about fashion. Then the queen produced a beautiful brush with gold filigree on it. "This is the finest brush I have ever used," the queen said.

"It's lovely," Violet answered.

The queen signaled, and a maid came forward and took the brush from her. "See what it does for your hair," the queen said.

Violet sat still as the maid approached her with the brush. She felt the bristles touch her hair and stroke downward. She tensed, waiting. Finally, she felt a small twinge. Violet cried out and put her hand to her head. "Ouch!"

She felt silly and awkward, but she tried to contort her face with pain even as she wished she knew how to cry on demand. With each passing test Violet felt more like a fool. She remembered joking with Richard about how a woman sensitive enough to please his parents couldn't possibly have the strength to bear children. Thinking about her competition, Violet was certain that at least half of the delicate princesses would die in childbirth, if they even survived the pregnancy.

"Oh, my dear, have you been injured?" the queen asked.

"It's nothing," Violet started to say, and then stammered to a stop. "Well, actually, yes, it does hurt. I think she pulled a hair from my head."

"I'm sorry, milady; it was very clumsy of me," the maid said. The woman moved away and handed the brush back to the queen.

"I hope you will feel better shortly."

"I hope so," Violet said through gritted teeth.

She couldn't believe Richard's mother actually thought she was still in pain.

"Perhaps you should go lie down."

"Thank you," Violet said, standing up. She turned to the door and then forced herself to stop and turn back. Violet didn't want the queen to suspect that she'd known what the test had been, since it had not been revealed at breakfast. "But Your Majesty, it can wait. I want to take the second test now."

For just a moment Violet thought she saw the hint of a smirk on the older woman's face, but it quickly disappeared. "Don't worry, my dear. You already have."

"Did I pass?" Violet asked.

The queen shook her head. "We'll let you know later tonight."

Violet returned to her room and tried not to worry about all the things that she wanted to fret about. She glanced over at Genevieve and noticed that the other girl looked pale.

"Are you okay?"

"I have a headache," Genevieve said, her voice strained.

Violet stared at her in disbelief. Could Genevieve be faking it? Surely having a single hair pulled couldn't actually have been debilitating?

"How come?"

"I don't know. I get them sometimes; I never know why."

Violet relaxed slightly. It was just a case of bad timing. "How did you do in today's test?"

Genevieve shook her head. "I'm still not sure what it was."

"It was strange," Violet offered, without saying more.

"As much as I hate to admit it, I don't think I'm going to feel like doing my own hair tonight?" Genevieve sighed.

Violet had no desire to try to duplicate one of the elaborate hairstyles she had seen at the castle during the last two days. "I can have your maids come and help in a little while."

"I'm sure they'd like that."

In the end Genevieve's entourage came traipsing

into the room, shooting haughty glances at Violet. They helped Genevieve get dressed while Violet wrestled with her own garment. At last Christine approached her. "Can I help you?" she asked Violet.

"No, I can manage," Violet said, trying to twist her arms far enough behind her to lace up the back of the dress.

"I'm sure you can manage, but you shouldn't have to."

Violet looked at the other girl. "I'm no better than you are," she said.

The maid shook her head. "You're a princess. There are just some tasks you can't do, or shouldn't do," she corrected herself.

Violet gave up with a sigh. "Thank you," she said as the girl laced her into the dress.

"You're welcome."

At last both Violet and Genevieve were dressed. Violet was wearing a white dress with silver trim. Staring in the mirror, she noticed how much more obvious her tanned skin was in contrast to the snowy white of the dress. She considered changing and then rolled her eyes in frustration. "I'm starting to think that all I ever do is eat and change clothes," Violet complained.

"Welcome to the life of a princess," Genevieve said with a tired smile. She was wearing a pale green dress that somehow seemed to emphasize the pallor of her skin. Even when she pinched her cheeks for color, it didn't seem to help. Violet sighed as she turned back to the mirror.

"Do you still have that headache?"

"Yes. Hopefully it will be gone by the morning."

When Violet entered the banquet hall, she was shocked to see that Celeste was already there, her head bandaged. "What happened?" Violet asked.

"The clumsy maid pulled a hair from my head, and I have been in agonizing pain ever since," she pouted.

"You can't be serious," Violet said.

"I guess I'm just too sensitive, not that you would understand." Celeste sighed dramatically. "If only I could be rough and coarse, like you," she said, her voice sickly sweet.

"Oh, I'd like to pull *all* your hair out," Violet hissed, lunging forward.

Celeste screamed and someone grabbed Violet by the shoulders. "No, Violet, don't give her what she wants," she heard Genevieve beg.

Violet glared at Celeste. "This isn't over," Violet said, her voice low enough that only the three of them could hear. Celeste rolled her eyes and then flounced off to her seat.

Genevieve pulled Violet into her seat. Everyone was looking at Violet. And she was shocked to see that Celeste was not the only one whose head was bandaged. Violet shook her head in disgust. It was bad enough that she had lied over the plucked hair causing her pain. With the rest of the contestants making such a fuss, it only made her job that much harder.

"Nobody could really be crippled from having one

hair pulled out," she whispered to Genevieve.

The other girl shrugged, clearly more interested in keeping a quarrel from breaking out than on the niceties of the competition. "You need to calm down. Picking a fight with Celeste would be more than enough reason for them to send you home for not being sensitive or delicate enough to marry Prince Richard."

Genevieve was right, and Violet knew it. It didn't stop her from wanting to dunk Celeste's face into her soup bowl, though.

"How can you be so calm?"

Genevieve smiled. "I just think of all the stories I'm going to tell about Celeste and some of the others when I get home. They'll be the greatest villains of all time, and they won't even know it."

Across the table the girl with the fake teeth appeared to be in great distress, as she had bandages that wrapped all the way around her head. For a moment Violet contemplated the stories that would be told about her and her teeth and started to feel a bit better.

Soon the remaining girls had assembled around the table. Violet looked expectantly toward the doorway, eager to see Richard. He was, after all, the reason she was putting up with Celeste and the others like her. Neither Richard nor his parents were anywhere to be seen, though. The steward strode to the head of the table and, after a brief consultation with one of the servants, drew the guests' attention.

"The king and queen send their apologies. They

will not be joining you tonight. One of their servants, Mary, became ill early this morning and has since passed on. In light of this tragedy they did not feel it was appropriate to celebrate this evening. They do, however, wish for you to enjoy yourselves despite their absence."

Violet felt ill. She hadn't known Mary well, but she had seemed a good woman. Her thoughts turned to her own mother, who was soon to be dead. Tears stung her eyes, and she signaled to the steward, who came over. "Excuse me, please. I have to go," Violet said.

He nodded, and she stood up, wiping her eyes.

A few other girls were also distraught. But the girl with the fake teeth said, "I don't get it. It was only a servant; why are people so upset?"

Violet fled toward the stairs. Back in her room she fell on her bed and began to cry.

"Violet, are you all right?"

She sat up to see Richard standing in the doorway. "You shouldn't be here," she said, wiping at her tears.

"I know, but I saw you run by looking terribly upset. Tell me what is troubling you."

"I was so sad to hear that Mary died. Then I started to think about my mother."

Richard approached Violet gingerly until he was standing next to her. "If you want, I can send a messenger to your father to see what word there is."

She was torn. She had just heard from Thomas that morning, but he had said she was failing.

"You would do that for me?" she asked, looking up at Richard.

"I would move heaven and earth for you," he said with a frown. "I don't like seeing you like this."

"I'm sorry. It's just been a lot to take."

"I didn't mean the tears. I meant, like this," Richard said, indicating the room and her dress. "It's not you."

"No, it's not," Violet said miserably. "I'm not a princess; I'm a farm girl, and that's what I want to be."

"Then why are you here?" Prince Richard asked, his eyes piercing her soul.

Violet couldn't lie to him. "I'm here because, as much as I want to be a farm girl, I want even more to be your wife."

Richard crossed the room to her in two strides, and the expression on his face was so fierce that she recoiled a moment. He reached out and grabbed Violet's arms and pulled her to his chest. He slid his right hand up behind her head and then kissed her hard. He held her so tightly Violet couldn't have moved even if she had wanted to.

The first time Richard had kissed her, standing in the field, his lips had been soft, the kiss gentle. This time it was intense. The onslaught made her gasp. She wrapped her arms around his neck and clung to him.

"Then be my wife, Violet. Come with me now, tonight. We'll go to Father Paul and have him marry us. No more games, no more challenges, just you and me and what we want."

Violet couldn't think. The room seemed to be

spinning crazily as he continued to kiss her lips and then began to move his way down to her throat. "Will you take me as your husband, Violet?"

Longing for him nearly overpowered her, but Violet managed to keep her wits.

"I will, but not like this. Not like thieves in the night. If I run away with you, I'll never have your parents' respect, and you will never regain your honor."

"I don't care."

"Maybe that's true, but I care, and someday you will too."

Richard kissed her again. From deep inside of her Violet called upon strength she didn't even know she had and stepped out of his embrace. "I love you, Richard, with all my heart, but for both of our sakes you need to leave right now."

He stood, fists clenched at his sides and fire smoldering in his eyes, and she was sure he was going to refuse. After what seemed an eternity his shoulders slumped. Without saying another word he turned and left.

CHAPTER NINE

Richard paced outside the castle and into the darkness, frustration flooding through him. He wished Violet had agreed to run away with him, but in his heart he knew that she was right. He didn't know what games his parents were playing, but it looked like he was going to have to play along for the time being.

Richard walked to the stables and spent some time grooming Baron. The stallion leaned into the brush and made contented sounds. For much of the last year they had been each other's only steady companions, and Richard had grown accustomed to talking to his horse.

"What am I going to do about her?" he asked the stallion. The horse nickered and nuzzled him, searching for a treat. "Sorry, boy, I'll bring you something tomorrow, I promise."

When Richard had finished grooming Baron, he gave him a pat on his neck before heading inside. It was time to find out what the next challenge was so that he could warn Violet.

Violet was still standing staring at the door, when Genevieve returned to the room. "Violet, is everything all right?"

Violet shook her head.

"Is it because of Mary?"

"It's a lot of things," Violet said. "Mary, my mother, this contest."

"If you don't mind my saying so," Genevieve began, "you've been wildly uncomfortable since you got here."

"That's true," Violet admitted.

"If you want to win the prince, be true to who you are. If he cares for you, that's what will impress him."

Violet closed her eyes and remembered the feeling of Richard's lips on hers. "Unfortunately, it's his parents I'm worried about impressing."

Genevieve waved a hand. "I've been thinking about it, and I'm pretty sure they're not as crazy as they appear to be."

"What do you mean?"

"These tests all seem so frivolous. I think there's something more going on than we know."

"Like a test within the test?"

"Exactly."

Violet walked over and fell back on her bed again with a groan.

"Great, as if I didn't have enough to worry about."

"I was trying to make you feel better," Genevieve pointed out.

A new idea occurred to Violet, and she sat up. "Did anyone ever announce who passed the test today?"

Genevieve shook her head and sat down beside Violet on the bed. "No, the steward said we would know in the morning. Several of us were sure there hadn't even been a test."

"And?" Violet asked.

"It turns out we each had an audience with the queen. She showed us a special hairbrush, her maid began to brush our hair, she yanked one of the hairs from our head, and then the queen sent us on our way."

"Me too. So, what does that mean, exactly?" Violet asked, anxious to keep her and Richard's secret.

"I think they were testing to see who was injured by it."

"Like Celeste," Violet said.

"Yes. When she started making such a big deal about it, I was pretty sure that the hair pulling was the test."

"Does anyone have any idea what to expect next?" Violet asked hopefully.

"None, so it seems."

"So what now?" Violet asked, more to herself than to Genevieve.

"There is nothing we can do except get some rest."

"I can't sleep yet." Violet sighed. "I think I'll go for a walk in the garden."

"Okay. I'll see you in the morning," Genevieve said.

Violet crossed to the armoire and took out the black cloak she had seen in it earlier. She draped the rich fabric around her and left the room. She wasn't completely sure where she was going, but Violet felt the need to be free of the castle walls.

Out in the gardens Violet began to walk contemplatively, breathing in the cool night air. She wandered farther than she and Genevieve had explored before. As silence stretched around her, Violet began to feel better.

What has happened to me? she wondered. Her life on the farm seemed so far away.

A sudden splash interrupted the quiet. Curious, Violet wandered deeper into the gardens, looking for the source of the sound. A wall of hedges rose on her left, looming in the dark. She touched it. It was the outer wall of the great maze that would be one of the contests during the Feasting. Violet had thought to enter the maze contest this year. Little had she guessed that she would be involved in a much more strenuous series of contests, to win not a ribbon but a husband.

Violet heard the splashing again, a little ways to her right. She turned and headed toward the sound. A few steps further on Violet found a large fountain. Standing in the middle of it was Arianna.

"Hello," Violet said quietly.

Arianna jumped and spun around, eyes wild.

But when she saw it was Violet, she relaxed slightly. "Hello," she answered tentatively.

Violet moved closer. Arianna's shoes were on the ground near the fountain. And Arianna stood in the middle of the pool, skirts gathered above her knees.

"I live near the ocean; I miss the water," Arianna said, lifting her chin as if defying Violet.

"I've never seen the ocean. What's it like?"

"Like . . . freedom," Arianna said, closing her eyes and spinning around. "Imagine standing in the surf and looking out and seeing only water. No land in sight. Just the blue of the ocean stretching to the horizon until it meets the blue of the sky."

"You make it sound wonderful," Violet said.

"It is."

"Is your mother really a mermaid?" Violet asked.

Arianna just smiled and stretched out her hand. "Join me."

Violet knew the proper thing to do would be to decline, but what had Genevieve just said, about being true to who she really was? Who she really was really wanted to jump in the fountain.

Violet kicked off her shoes, took off her cloak, hiked up her skirts, and climbed into the fountain, gasping as the cold water hit her calves. Arianna clapped her hands and danced, spinning and twirling.

"Don't be afraid to let your dress get wet," she said.

"It's not technically my dress," Violet said.

"Even better!" Arianna laughed.

Violet couldn't help but laugh too. "I don't think I'm even a real princess," she said.

"Wonderful," Arianna said, throwing her arms toward the sky as she spun.

"Up until a couple of days ago I lived on a farm," Violet said, spinning around herself.

"That's amazing. What is that like?"

"I love it. Hard work, sunshine, simple food, no servants or fancy clothes that I can't get wet," Violet said, laughing harder as she danced in the fountain.

"Then why are you even here?" Arianna asked.

"Because I was crazy enough to fall in love with a prince. How silly is that?"

Arianna stopped spinning, and her face turned serious. "It's not silly at all. Love is never silly. It is beautiful, terrible, unexpected, uplifting, heartbreaking. It is everything but silly."

Violet blinked in surprise at the sudden transition. "You really are in love with a werewolf, aren't you?"

"Descendant. It's complicated," Arianna said. She smiled. "But that's love!"

An hour later Violet crept back into her room, her wet skirts heavy as she tried to hold them up off of the floor. There was a candle burning on the desk, and Genevieve was sitting up in a dressing gown, staring at her.

"Genevieve, you're awake," Violet said in surprise, aware that something was wrong.

Genevieve held out a parchment to her. "A dog came for you."

"I can explain," Violet said quickly, taking the letter from her.

"You don't have to explain anything," Genevieve said. "You love him; he loves you. I think that's great."

Violet threw her arms around her. "Thank you."

Genevieve laughed and pushed Violet away. "You didn't tell me you were going swimming."

"Sorry! Next time I'll take you with me."

Violet pulled off her soggy dress and changed into her nightgown. "So, what did the dog's letter have to say?"

"Once I figured out it was for you, I didn't read any further," Genevieve said.

When she had finished changing, Violet opened the parchment and read:

My love. Tomorrow they are testing the sensitivity of your skin, particularly your feet. You will be asked to walk across grass. The intended result is that the blades of grass will cut your feet. There are some berries in the kitchen that you could use to stain the bottom of your feet so it would look like blood. Forever yours, Richard.

"How sensitive are the bottoms of your feet?" Violet asked, handing Genevieve the letter.

"Terribly sensitive. My father used to tickle them when I was a child, and I would just go crazy laughing. Why?"

"For the challenge tomorrow we will be asked to walk barefoot over the grass in expectation that it will cut our feet."

Genevieve wrinkled her nose up. "Who would think up such a challenge?"

"Richard's parents, apparently."

"That doesn't seem right to me."

"Me either, but what can we do?"

"We can refuse," Genevieve said.

Violet sighed. "You can, but I'm not willing to give up on marrying Richard."

"Then it's off to the kitchens with you," Genevieve said, scanning the letter.

The next morning at breakfast the royal family was once again present. The king, queen, and prince all ate quickly, Violet noted, and soon Richard and his mother excused themselves. The king then stood and called for attention.

"I apologize for our absence last night. We do, however, have the results of the second test. Four of you are now out of the running and may go or stay as you wish."

None of the princesses were girls Violet knew. The first one bounced up from the table when her name was called, unable to hide a grin. The other three rose more slowly, faces solemn. Violet heaved a sigh of relief. She was still in the competition.

"After breakfast the rest of you may assemble in the gardens," the king announced before he, too, left the room.

"We're going to be able to see each other compete this time," Goldie guessed.

"What's wrong, Arianna?" Genevieve asked.

Violet looked at the girl with the silvery hair, who sat by Genevieve. Arianna's brow was furrowed and she looked troubled.

"Can someone explain to me what the last test was?" she asked.

"You had to feel great pain if a single hair was pulled," another girl said.

Arianna shook her head. "I don't think that was it."

"Why not?" Violet asked.

Arianna looked at her. "I talked with the queen like the rest of you, and her maid brushed my hair, but I never noticed her pulling a hair."

"Are you sure?" Violet asked sharply.

"Yes," Arianna replied. "She brushed my hair for about five minutes, and I didn't feel anything."

"There must have been some mistake then," Genevieve said slowly.

"I don't think there's a mistake," Arianna said. "I think they don't want us to know what the real tests are."

Violet glanced over at Genevieve. "We were thinking the same thing last night," she said.

"This is ridiculous," Goldie countered. "Why would they go to such lengths to hide what they were doing?"

"Maybe so no one could cheat," Violet said guiltily.

"But how? I mean, none of us are likely to tell each other what we've discovered. We are all competing against each other. I mean, I think I was the first one to take the silk thread test, and I didn't tell any of you that the silk threads were right, right, left, right," Goldie said.

"You mean left, left, right, left," Violet corrected.

"You're both wrong. It was left, right, left, right," Arianna said.

"Actually, it was a trick test," Genevieve said very quietly. "Every single thread was silk."

Violet looked sharply at her. "Really?"

She nodded.

"Is it possible that they changed it each time, so we couldn't get the answer from each other?" Goldie asked.

Violet shook her head. There would have been no way for Richard to accurately predict how the threads would be when it came her turn, if that were the case. "How many of you do embroidery?"

"Not me," Goldie said.

"Or me," Arianna answered.

"You know I do," Genevieve said.

"So you were the only one who could have possibly told the difference between the cotton and the silk threads."

"What does it all mean?" Goldie asked.

"It means we have no idea what the real challenges are testing us on," Violet whispered.

There was silence for a moment as the four let that sink in.

"That changes everything," Goldie finally said.

Around them the others were finishing breakfast

and getting up from the table. "Time to head outside," Arianna said.

Violet stood up, palming a couple of berries from her plate as she did so. The others didn't notice, and together they left the table and headed into the gardens.

Violet showed Genevieve the berries and offered her one. The other girl shook her head. Soon they were on a grassy expanse where the other girls, Richard, his parents, the steward, and a few servants waited.

"Princesses, for this challenge we will test the sensitivity of your skin. You will remove your shoes and walk barefoot across this expanse of grass," the steward said.

"To what end?" Arianna asked.

"We expect that the grass will cut your feet if they are delicate."

One of the girls Violet didn't know very well fell to the ground in a faint.

Arianna crossed her arms over her chest. "I refuse."

"Are you afraid, my dear?" the king asked.

"No, I am not. There is no point in participating, because I already know the outcome. I swim in the ocean at home. I walk on pebbles and rocks and sand. The grass will be as nothing to my feet, and I will walk across uninjured. If you think that all true princesses bleed easily, and are soft and weak, then it is best that I withdraw now."

Violet watched in fascination as the king and queen whispered together for a moment.

The king turned back. "We respect your choice to decline the challenge. We ask that you respect our request that you stay at least until tomorrow."

Arianna nodded and stepped back. Violet gazed at her with admiration for having spoken up. Still, Arianna did not wish to win the competition and marry Richard, so she lost nothing by refusing the challenge.

"Who would like to go first?" the steward asked.

Genevieve stepped forward. "I will go."

"Are your feet also strong?" the king asked.

Genevieve shook her head. "No, quite the opposite. I have never walked barefoot anywhere, and I expect to be injured."

"You may proceed."

Genevieve slipped off her shoes and began to walk across the grass with slow, pained steps. When she turned to walk back, Violet could see the tears rolling down Genevieve's cheeks. Violet ran to her friend and stopped her. Violet bent and picked her up as she would a sack of grain.

"I can do it," Genevieve protested.

"And you have done it," Violet said, carrying her back. "The steward only said you had to walk across; he said nothing about walking back."

When they had returned to the cluster of princesses, Violet set Genevieve down gently. The bottoms of both of Genevieve's feet were actually bleeding.

"Why did you do this to yourself when you don't even want to win?" Violet whispered.

Genevieve smiled and whispered back, "To take the focus off of you and what you're about to do."

A couple of servants rushed forward with bandages, and Violet left Genevieve to their care.

Violet stood and watched as several others crossed the grass. Several suffered some sort of injury, but none as severe as Genevieve's. When it was Goldie's turn, Violet watched her take off her shoes and was stunned to see her scratch the bottom of her left foot with her fingernails. By the time Goldie came limping back, blood had oozed from the wound.

Then Violet and Celeste were the only ones left. Celeste went first, and she had barely gone two steps when she cried out and sank to the ground. Servants hurried forward to help her stand. "I can do it," she said breathlessly. She took several more steps and then collapsed, needing to be carried back.

Violet took a deep breath. The berries were still in her hand. She looked over at Richard, who nodded encouragement. Then she looked at his parents and wondered what they possibly hoped to accomplish with such a test. Violet didn't want to do it. It was ridiculous. She couldn't pretend to be something she wasn't any longer. Violet prepared to slip off her shoes and walk across the grass. She glanced over at Genevieve and hesitated. The other girl had sacrificed so that Violet would have the chance to fake her own injury and pass the test. If she refused, then Genevieve had injured herself for naught.

Violet bent, pulled off her shoes, and smashed

the berries in her hand onto the bottom of each foot. Then she stood and walked as calmly as she could across the grass and back. She briefly displayed the bottom of each foot and then hastily put back on her slippers. Then she met Genevieve's gaze, and the two shared a grim smile.

Dinner that night was brief, as many of the girls just wanted to rest from the day's ordeal. Three more girls, including the one who had fainted before she could walk across the grass, were put out of the running. To everyone's surprise Arianna was not one of them. This confirmed for Violet that the challenges were a pretense and not the real test. Violet still had no idea what the real tests could be; all she knew was that ten princesses and three tests were all that remained.

Violet was ready with some table scraps for Duke when he padded into the room. "Good boy," she whispered as she took the parchment from him. He eagerly gobbled down the food she presented him. Violet sat down at the table, lit the candle, and began to read.

Violet. I can't find out anything about tomorrow's test. Keep your eyes open and expect anything. I'll try to help if I can. Yours, Richard.

CHAPTER TEN

Violet barely slept, tossing and turning all night. When she awoke, she couldn't shake the fear that had plagued her all night. This was only the fourth test of six, and she had no idea what it was, much less how to pass it.

Richard and his parents were absent at breakfast, which was considerably less elaborate than it had been other mornings. Each girl had a bowl of stew set before her. The food was hot and bland. It reminded her of many stews that she had had at home, and Violet ate hungrily.

Around her, the others made faces as they nibbled at the food. "The carrots taste okay," Goldie finally said.

"You have carrots? Where?" Genevieve asked, craning her head to see Goldie's bowl.

As breakfast came to an end, Violet couldn't help

but wonder why no one had mentioned anything about the next test. When a servant came to clear her dish, Violet asked where the steward was.

The man gave her a shrug and an apologetic smile but said nothing. She glanced around and discovered that none of the servants would meet her eyes.

"Something doesn't seem right here," she said, turning to Genevieve.

Genevieve looked pale, and sweat was beading on her forehead. "Something doesn't seem right here," she echoed, eyes glassy.

"Are you okay?" Violet asked in alarm.

"I don't think any of us are," Goldie said.

Violet glanced over and saw that she, too, looked sick.

"I think I should have gone home yesterday morning," Arianna said through lips that trembled.

Violet glanced up and down the table and saw that every girl looked terrible except for Celeste. "What's wrong with them?" she asked her.

Celeste sneered. "They ate the food."

"But so did I, and I'm fine."

"Then you must be used to eating peasant food. I wouldn't have served that to a dog."

Violet trembled with rage as she stared at the heir of Lore. She glanced around, and there was no one in the room other than them and the sick princesses. Violet rose from her seat. She could teach Celeste some manners. She could send the princess of Lore running from Cambria. No one was watching, and she would never have a better opportunity.

Violet approached Celeste. "You've pushed me once too often," she said.

"And what are you going to do about it?" Celeste sneered.

"Let me show you," Violet said, clenching her fists at her side.

Before she could strike out at Celeste, a sobbing sound distracted Violet. One of the girls was on her hands and knees, wincing in pain.

There were still no servants in sight. "We have to help them," Violet said, turning back to Celeste.

Celeste was staring at the stew still in front of her.

"Are you listening to me?" Violet asked. "They're sick; we have to help them."

"The food made them sick," Celeste said in a monotone. "It is peasant food. Their stomachs can't handle it."

"Then we need to help them."

"You don't understand," Celeste said, looking up at Violet with slightly glazed eyes. "This is the test."

Celeste grabbed her bowl of stew and poured it into her mouth.

"What are you doing?" Violet cried, trying to snatch the bowl away from her.

Celeste twisted so Violet couldn't reach it, and a moment later set the nearly empty bowl on the table. "I'm going to be sick," Celeste groaned.

"The stew couldn't have hit your stomach yet," Violet protested.

"Not that; the taste," Celeste said before sliding onto the floor in distress.

Violet stared at Celeste, disbelieving, then turned her attention to the others in the banquet hall. Several girls clutched their stomachs in pain, a couple other girls were crying, and at least one had passed out in her chair. And despite everything Violet had thought and felt and feared, she knew then that she might dress like them, even learn to act like them, but she would never truly be one of them.

Violet turned and hurried toward the kitchens. Her arrival there stopped all the servants in their tracks. Violet grabbed the woman who seemed to be in charge, noting that she wouldn't meet her eyes either. *They all knew the food would hurt the girls,* she realized. "Please help me. I need something to soothe the princesses' stomachs. There's a root Father Paul sometimes uses."

Before Violet could begin to describe it, one of the other cooks handed her a small bowl. Inside were cuttings of the plant Violet needed. "Thank you," she said. "I'm also going to need towels and water."

A few of the servants started to gather supplies at Violet's request, as Violet dashed back to the hall. Kneeling down beside the first girl to have gotten sick, Violet said, "Look at me," shaking her shoulder.

The girl did as she was told. Her eyes were wide in fear, and she was sweating and shaking uncontrollably. "How much did you eat?"

"Didn't eat that much," she mumbled.

"Okay, good. Have this anyway."

The girl swallowed the piece of the root, and then Violet signaled to one of the servants that had followed her from the kitchen. The woman scurried over, eyes wide.

"I want you to help her get cleaned up, and then move her somewhere and make her more comfortable. I don't think you should try taking her to her room yet; she looks too weak to make it up the stairs. Do you understand?"

The servant nodded. "Yes, milady."

Violet then moved over to Celeste, who was groaning on the floor. "Celeste, eat this," Violet said, handing her a bit of the root. Celeste grimaced and then slowly put it in her mouth and began chewing.

Violet stood and moved over to one of the boys from the kitchen. She handed him half a dozen clippings from the plant. "Go to all the ladies on that side of the table; make sure each one of them eats one of these."

"Yes," he said, moving toward Goldie.

Violet found Genevieve, who looked worse than many of the others. Her friend's skin was even paler than usual, and she was sweating and gasping as though she were having trouble breathing. Violet was able to help her eat the root. Then she moved on to administer to the others.

A minute later Arianna staggered up to Violet. "Go lie down," Violet ordered.

"No, I'm good. I want to help."

Violet sized her up for a moment. Of the group Arianna seemed to have the strongest constitution. "Go and see to Genevieve. I'm really worried about her," Violet confessed. She handed her the last piece of root. "She's already had one, but . . ."

"I understand," Arianna said before moving off.

Violet paused to assess the situation. Of the nine girls who were sick three, including Celeste, had been moved to makeshift beds on the far side of the hall. Four others, including Goldie, were still in the throes of being ill. She could hear Goldie wail something about never eating carrots again.

Arianna was shaky but generously caring for Genevieve, who seemed to have passed out from the pain in her stomach. Violet shook her head. Poor Genevieve. She was undoubtedly the most sensitive princess in the room, certainly the one with the worst luck. She felt a wave of fear wash over her. If the grass had made Genevieve's feet bleed, could the stew do permanent damage or even kill her? It seemed ridiculous, but before meeting Genevieve there had been a lot of things she found unbelievable that had been proved true.

As much as Violet wanted to soothe her friend, she realized there was nothing she could do for Genevieve that Arianna was not already doing. She turned and walked to the far end of the room to check on the three girls recuperating there.

"How are they?" she asked the woman overseeing the group.

"Better. Should I give them a little bread or something to eat?"

Violet shook her head. "Pass the word. Make sure they don't eat anything for at least a couple of hours until their stomachs have settled."

Celeste and one of the other girls were lying quietly, eyes closed and faces pale. The third was weeping openly, and Violet knelt beside her and put her hand on her back.

"Is there anything I can do for you?" Violet asked.

"I just want to go home."

Violet didn't know what to say, so she just stayed with her for a couple of minutes, rubbing her back and trying to quiet her. Finally, the girl's sobbing faded. Violet wished she could go home and hold her mother and comfort her. She wished she could give her a root and make her better. She wrestled with her own exhaustion and finally went to check on the others who were still sick.

They were doing better except for Genevieve. At least they had managed to wake her.

"Goldie, how are you doing?" Violet asked.

"I feel like I want to die," Goldie moaned.

"That's terrible!"

"Actually, it's an improvement. A couple of minutes ago I thought I had died," Goldie said, coughing.

Violet winced. She thought of her mother and struggled to keep back the tears. She patted Goldie on the shoulder.

Two hours later everyone was starting to feel

better. The girls were worn out, disheveled, but no longer violently ill. Even Genevieve seemed to be on the mend.

Violet finally took a moment to sit down and wipe the sweat from her forehead. Although the food hadn't made her sick, taking care of the others had exhausted her. What she wanted most was to take a bath and to get out into the fresh air. While Violet contemplated taking a short walk outside while her patients were stable, the steward put in an appearance.

He glanced around the hall and then made his way over to Violet.

"How is everyone?" he asked her.

She grimaced. "Not well, but improving. It seems that the stomach of a princess is sensitive as well."

He nodded. "That is the general idea."

She glared at him. "Some might think these tests funny, but people are getting hurt. This needs to stop."

It sounded like a threat, Violet knew, but she didn't bother to explain herself. His eyes widened in momentary dismay, and the steward took a step back. "It is out of my hands, milady," he said.

She stood up. Violet didn't want to engage in any more conversation for fear she would get angry. That would surely get her kicked out of the castle, but she was pretty sure that was a certainty anyway. Violet glanced over his shoulder and restrained herself, though, when she saw the royal family enter.

The queen had a kerchief covering her nose and mouth. Both Richard and his father, upon seeing the sick girls and disarray of the room, looked slightly ill. The steward scurried over to them. He whispered a few words she couldn't hear, and then the king nodded.

"My apologies. It seems you have been unfortunately served some rather unwholesome food," the king began.

Violet glared as she crossed her arms. He made it sound like an accident, when it so clearly had not been. And the stew wasn't bad; it just wasn't what they were used to.

"In light of the current situation I think it only fair to ask each of you a question. Do you want to continue on with the tests or withdraw?"

There was murmuring amongst all the girls as the implication of his words sank in. The king was giving them a choice: quit the field of competition or continue on and risk the consequences. Given that they had been intentionally fed food that made them ill, there was nothing to make them believe that continuing in the competition would be a safe course of action. What would the next two tests bring?

Violet glanced at Genevieve. The other girl had been so sick Violet had actually worried for her life. How could she trust that the final two tests wouldn't get someone killed?

The king turned toward Celeste, who was nearest him. "Princess Celeste, do you withdraw or do you continue?"

"I continue," Celeste said.

"Princess Lena?"

"Withdraw."

Again there was murmuring from the other girls.

"Princess Angela?"

"Withdraw."

"Princess Goldie?" the king asked.

"I will continue," Goldie said, voice shaking.

"Princess Ruth?"

"Continue."

"Princess Evaline?"

"Continue."

"Princess Arianna?"

Arianna stood up and bowed. "I choose to withdraw."

Violet stared at her. She knew Arianna didn't want to win, but it still surprised her that she had withdrawn.

"Princess Cora?"

"Withdraw."

"Princess Genevieve?"

"I wish to withdraw," Genevieve croaked.

"Princess Violet?"

Violet set her jaw. She had not come so far or endured this much not to continue, no matter the cost.

"I will continue," she said.

The king nodded. "Very well. Princesses Celeste, Goldie, Ruth, Evaline, and Violet will continue on to the next test. The rest of you may leave if you like, but you are certainly welcome to stay and observe the proceedings."

Violet looked at Richard and realized that he was just as upset by what had happened as she was. She gave him a slight nod and hoped that he knew she didn't blame him.

Servants began to help the princesses to their feet and to their rooms. Violet joined Arianna, Genevieve, and Goldie. Violet noticed that Arianna's pale skin was flushed a dark, angry red.

Arianna's eyes flashed as she spoke. "This is intolerable. I participated in their little games, but no more. The king and queen of Cambria should just be grateful I am not taking this poisoning as a declaration of war. It will, however, be many years before the people of Aster consider an alliance with Cambria."

"It is poor taste indeed given that their predecessors were assassinated," Genevieve said.

"Although it would have served Lore right if Celeste had died," Goldie said.

"I can't believe you withdrew," Violet said to Genevieve.

"Sure you can," Genevieve answered with a smile. "Because you know deep down that sooner or later one of these insane tests would have crippled me."

"You are amazingly fragile," Arianna said.

"Thank you, I think."

"I want to withdraw, but I can't," Goldie said.

"There is still danger that my uncle will try to overthrow me and claim the throne for himself. I need an alliance with Cambria. What about you, though?" Goldie asked Violet.

Arianna rolled her eyes. "There's no way she's going to withdraw. She's in love with Richard."

Goldie's eyes widened. "I had no idea. I guess I shouldn't be surprised; he is incredibly desirable, not just because of his position but because of his character." She bit her lip. "You have been very kind, and I respect your feelings for the prince, but I won't withdraw."

"It's okay," Violet said. "Besides, we were competitors first, friends second. And whatever happens here, I hope that the latter can still be true."

"It is agreed," Goldie said.

"We can be sure that Celeste will never give up. She wants the throne too badly. Even if she could be dissuaded, her parents would still push her," Genevieve said.

"Does anyone know much about Ruth or Evaline?" Arianna asked.

They all shook their heads. "I wish there was some way to get them to drop out," Goldie said.

"I'd love to continue this discussion," Arianna said, "but could we please do it out in the fresh air?"

Violet smiled. "I was thinking something similar."

"I could use a bath," Genevieve said.

"Well, if you're not afraid of a little cold water, I've got a great idea," Arianna said mischievously.

"You wouldn't!" Violet said, laughing.

"Watch me. After that stunt they'll be lucky if I only bathe in the fountain," Arianna said stubbornly.

"What are the two of you talking about?" Goldie asked.

Arianna held out a hand to Goldie as Violet helped Genevieve stand. "Come with us and find out."

CHAPTER ELEVEN

It was Richard who found them all in the fountain. Genevieve was perched daintily on the side with only her feet dangling in the water. Arianna had submerged herself entirely, and Violet and Goldie were splashing each other and laughing.

"What are you doing?" Richard asked in a shocked voice.

"Celebrating," Genevieve answered.

"Celebrating what?"

"That Genevieve and I are no longer in the competition," Arianna said, surfacing and spitting water out of her mouth like the fish that topped the fountain.

"Well, two of you are still in the competition, so make sure you don't let my parents catch you," he warned.

"I think Prince Richard is too serious," Arianna said. "What do you think?"

"Yes, definitely too serious," Genevieve said, her eyes wide.

Violet hadn't felt so free since leaving the farm. She'd been so focused on winning she'd forgotten to enjoy life along the way. She took careful aim with Arianna and then splashed Richard.

He yelped and jumped away from the fountain's edge. Violet started laughing and wasn't sure she'd ever stop. All the pressure of the last few days seemed to slip away.

"Okay, all this excitement is a little too much for Genevieve," Arianna said with a grin. "Come on, let's go change into clean, dry clothes."

Genevieve rolled her eyes. "I have enough people telling me what to do," she protested. Still, she stood up, retrieved her slippers, and started walking with Arianna toward the castle.

Goldie looked suddenly uncomfortable. "I think I'll go with them," she said, splashing out of the pool. "We've already had too much sun and are sure to be burnt."

"That just leaves you I'll have to chase out of the fountain," Richard said with a smile.

"You'll have to catch me first," Violet said.

She splashed him again, and to her surprise Richard jumped into the fountain. Violet squealed and backed away, trying to splash water in his face. He chased after her, water spraying around him, his boots slowing him down. He finally dashed straight through the cascading water tumbling from the fish sculpture and finally caught her. The laughter died on her lips.

He leaned in and kissed her. Violet put her arms around his neck, and he wrapped his around her waist. He lifted her up into the air, and for a moment the world seemed to fade away. There were only the two of them and the kiss that she wanted to last forever. How long it did last, she didn't know. Violet just knew that when Richard pulled away, it felt like her heart would break.

"I love you," he whispered, and her heart mended. "I can't believe how much you're putting up with for me."

"So are the others."

"No, they're doing it for their parents or for their kingdoms and the alliance they hope to forge. But you, you're doing this just for me. Why?"

"I love you too," she answered. "I don't care who knows it or what I have to do to prove it."

"You have proved it a hundred times over. It's I who should be proving my love to you," he breathed.

"And how would you prove this love?" she asked.

"I would do anything for you. I would swim across an ocean to find you. I would walk through fire to be with you. I would sacrifice my life for your happiness."

"I think I'd settle for another kiss," she said.

"You shall have all you could ever want," he said, before kissing her again.

When he pulled away again, he said, "You're shivering."

"Because of you."

Richard smiled gently. "I wish that were true. I'm afraid the cold and the water have more to do with it than I do. You should go inside and change."

"I don't want this moment to end," Violet said, a sudden fear gripping her heart. "What if it's our last?"

"Dearest Violet, it is only our first."

"Promise me."

"I promise you. Whatever it takes, whatever I must do, we will be together, always."

He helped her out of the fountain and she pulled on her shoes. When she turned to look at him, he was smiling.

"What?" she asked.

He shook his head. "I have a surprise for you."

"What is it?"

"I can't tell you. You'll just have to be patient."

"I'm tired of waiting . . . for everything," she confessed.

"Trust me, it will be worth it."

She glanced toward the castle, the polished stone glistening in the noonday sun. It was still so strange to be living there, even if it was only for a few days. "There's so much I don't know," she admitted.

"About what?" he asked.

"About everything. Life, you, being a lady. I don't know how I am supposed to eat or talk or be a princess."

"Violet, you don't have to try to be *like* a princess; you *are* a princess."

"How can you be so sure?" Violet asked him. She

was shaking harder now, but it wasn't from the cold and the wet. Violet loved Richard; she wanted to be with him. But she wondered if he would regret being with someone like her, even if she did win his parents' bizarre competition. What if he would be better off with someone like Goldie? The two could really help each other, could probably learn to love each other. Violet felt tears begin to streak her cheeks. She wiped them away angrily. She had never cried as much in her life as she had in the past few days.

"The princess of Cambria vanished during the attack," he said, eyes burning brightly.

"Really?" she asked, heart beginning to pound. Maybe it really was true. Maybe she really was a princess. A moment later doubt washed over her.

"How do you know that the child even lived, or that I'm her?"

Violet looked to him to somehow explain, to make it right. Instead she saw doubt flicker across his face as well.

"What is it?" she asked, fear tugging at her.

Prince Richard bit his lip. "She could have been killed. Or she could be you."

"Or?" she asked, sensing there was something else.

"Or she could have been kidnapped and raised in Lore."

Celeste. Celeste could actually be the true princess of Cambria, raised by Lorian enemies and ignorant of her birth. Violet's knees gave way, and she collapsed onto the ground. It was so terrible it might even be true. And if it was, the only way Richard's parents could secure the throne would be by ensuring he married Celeste. Maybe the tests were so strange *because* they knew Celeste was the rightful princess of Cambria and they had to make sure that Celeste passed every one.

Richard knelt beside Violet.

"I could not bear it if you married her," Violet admitted. Staring at him, though, she knew it was inevitable. Either Celeste was the true princess of the kingdom and Richard would have to marry her, or Celeste was the daughter of Cambria's greatest possible enemy, and to keep the peace Richard would have to marry her.

"But that's what's going to happen," she continued. "I have to go. I can't stay here and watch."

Prince Richard grabbed Violet's shoulders and shook her, panic edging into his voice. "Violet, don't you give up on me! You've come so far; you can't quit now. I love you, and I will do whatever it takes to be with you. You're the one who refused to run away with me earlier; don't run away from me now."

"But your parents—"

"My parents are playing some game. I don't know what it is. What I do know is that you're one of the few still standing. We have to trust that that means something."

"But Celeste—"

"Nothing is going to come between us, do you understand me?"

Violet nodded her head slowly, his intensity overwhelming and strengthening her. Prince Richard helped Violet to her feet and she leaned against him for a moment. "I've never felt so helpless," she said.

He smiled. "And you thought you weren't a princess."

While he was trying to make her laugh, Violet just couldn't get there. She shook herself slightly and then stood up straight. "I can walk by myself."

"Are you sure?" Richard asked doubtfully.

"Yes."

"Well, you better get inside quick; you're getting a chill."

She nodded and hurried back toward the warmth and safety of the room she shared with Genevieve. Richard was right—the wind that was blowing and the cold water had conspired to give her a chill.

But deep in the back of her mind she knew it wasn't cold, or love, that made her shiver.

It was fear.

Genevieve was content, sipping a hot beverage, curled up in a chair, listening to Arianna telling her stories of Aster, when Violet arrived back at their room.

"You simply must come to visit me," Arianna urged. "We could have wonderful adventures."

Genevieve smiled sadly. "My parents don't approve of adventures."

"Then we won't tell them we're having adventures. You can come for my wedding."

"The werewolf?" Genevieve asked in surprise.

"The son of a werewolf, well, former werewolf," Arianna said with a sigh.

Violet shed her wet dress and began changing into a pretty red one. "How can you be engaged already?" she asked, relieved to talk about something that didn't involve Richard or Celeste.

"Simple," Arianna said. "My parents agreed that if I came home without a husband, I could marry David. It's a good match, not as strong as one with Cambria would have been, but it is suitable nonetheless."

"Congratulations," Violet said.

"What's wrong?" Genevieve asked. "Didn't things go well with Richard?"

Violet couldn't hide her expression of surprise. It was uncanny how quickly Genevieve could pick up on her moods.

"Richard was wonderful. But now here I am again, and all the uncertainty is back. I don't know how much longer I can do this," Violet admitted, not yet ready to say more.

Genevieve crossed her arms. "As long as it takes."

"Would you like us to poison Celeste for real?" Arianna asked, a little too eagerly.

"No," Violet said. "But thanks for the offer. Are you two going to be leaving soon?" Violet asked, suddenly realizing just how much she would miss them both.

"No, we plan to stay to see you win your prince," Genevieve said.

"And in case you decide to change your mind

about poisoning Celeste," Arianna added with a glint in her eye.

"Remind me never to eat anything you've prepared," Violet said, her mood lightening.

Arianna grinned. "You're fairly safe. I've never made a meal. I wouldn't know where to begin."

"You know, I've been trying to understand what these challenges are really testing," Genevieve said. "I think I figured out the last one."

"It was testing who was stupid enough to risk getting seriously injured by continuing on?" Arianna asked.

"No," Genevieve grimaced, glancing quickly at Violet.

"Sorry, Violet. I meant no offense to your intelligence. You're in love, which explains all kinds of things," Arianna said with a toss of her silvery hair.

"Thank you, I think," Violet said.

"So, what was it testing?" Arianna asked more seriously.

"I think it was significant that we were each allowed to choose whether or not to continue. It's almost like our ability to persevere in the face of danger and difficulty was being observed."

"Then you and I failed," Arianna said.

"Would they test something like that?" Violet asked. It must be difficult to be a ruler, but she had no basis for comparison. Her parents, the people in her village, even she herself never had any choice but to persevere. If you didn't persevere, you didn't eat, you didn't survive.

Arianna looked at her curiously. "Is that really your question?"

"Yes, I guess it is."

"Of course they would. Being a queen is hard work. You have to put the entire kingdom before yourself. You have to push yourself to work long and hard, making sure complaints are heard and resolved, keeping the peace, protecting against invasion, figuring out year after year how to protect, feed, and shelter your subjects. And when a queen has a bad day, she can't just go to bed and pray for the next. She needs to work through her problems, face them at that moment. Lives are at stake with every decision, every breath. I'm sure Richard's parents want to know that whoever they choose for their son will have the strength, the fortitude to be by his side. To keep going no matter what the cost, the personal risk—that is what we do."

Arianna paused, and Genevieve said quietly, "Look at Goldie. She knows her uncle is going to try to kill her so that he can be king. A normal person might run away, or let him have the throne. A ruler can't run, and she can't back down. She's going to stay and fight for the good of her kingdom. In the end it might cost Goldie her life, but she knows that, and she perseveres anyway."

Tears began to stream down Violet's cheeks. She couldn't imagine being in Goldie's position. No one would want to kill a farmer's daughter. She had nothing someone else would covet so deeply.

"How does she do it?" Violet asked.

"She does it because she has to," Goldie said from the doorway.

Violet went and hugged her. Goldie hugged her back, tight.

"I'm sorry, my hair's still wet," Violet realized at last, trying to pull away.

"I don't care," Goldie said, hugging her tighter. Her shoulders began to shake, and Violet realized she was crying as well.

"I promise I will do anything I can to help you," Violet said. It wasn't much, but it was all she had to give. In her heart Violet knew that a week's time might find her back on her family's farm, castles and gowns and princes a distant memory, like a dream of someone else's life.

The next morning Violet waited anxiously with Goldie, Celeste, Ruth, and Evaline in a small room in the castle. She had no idea what the challenge was to be. She had waited up half the night, but Duke had never come with a message for her.

Finally, the queen entered, alone. "Good morning," she greeted them.

"Good morning," Violet answered with the others.

"One of the most priceless things a princess or a queen has is her beauty," the queen began. "We are taught from a young age to guard this beauty jealously and to let nothing mar it."

Around her Violet saw heads nodding, and she

fought back a sigh. Yet another princess rule that meant nothing to her.

"We are told that we don't expose our skin to the sun, because it will burn and it will age us prematurely. We are told that soft, white skin is beautiful and skin darkened by the sun is not."

Violet looked down at her own tanned hands and grimaced. She wasn't sure what the queen was leading up to, but she was certain it was going to be another task that would be impossible for her to accomplish by normal means.

"So here is the fifth test. You will each put your hand out one of these windows and leave it there for a quarter of an hour. We will then check to see which of you have burned skin."

Ruth and Goldie gasped, and Celeste groaned.

"I can't," Evaline said through pursed lips.

"But you must, or forfeit," the queen said.

Evaline shook her head. "I can't. I won't. I'm going home."

"Then go," the queen said, standing aside to let Evaline pass.

Violet stared after her. Was it really so much worse than everything that had gone before? She couldn't believe it.

"You may begin," Queen Martha said.

Each of them moved to a window and put her hand out into the bright sunlight. Fifteen minutes later the girls were allowed to pull their hands back inside. Then they followed the queen to another room, one without windows.

"You may wait in here," the queen said. "In an hour I will return to check your hands."

The queen left, and Violet took one of the chairs, staring glumly at her hand. Violet couldn't sit still, though, and began to pace. Even in the dim candlelight Violet could see the sunburns on the other girls' hands.

How can I make my hand look burned when it's not? she wondered. There was nothing in the room to stain it red or pink. Violet continued to pace, turning the notion over in her mind. *Maybe I should stop worrying about the sunburn and focus on figuring out what the real test is.*

Violet thought of everything Genevieve had said about the tests behind the challenges. Yesterday had been about perseverance. From what the queen had said, a princess would consider it terrible to get a sunburn. *Why? Because they think it mars their beauty. So, then, why allow it to happen? Because they want to win. And what are they proving?*

Violet had to win; she was so close to the end of the contest, and the memory of Richard's lips on hers and their connection spurred her on. In the light of a new day she didn't care who Celeste was or wasn't. All she knew was that she loved Richard and she had to try. He had been so passionate when they kissed. What had Richard said about proving his love? Could the princesses risking their beauty prove something to the king and queen? Then, suddenly, something Richard had said came to her: *I would sacrifice my life for your happiness.*

Violet stopped pacing. That was it! King Charles and Queen Martha wanted to know if the girls would sacrifice their beauty to win Richard. Sacrifice. That was what it all came down to. Rulers had to sacrifice their own desires. Violet glanced over at Goldie. Sometimes they had to sacrifice their own lives.

If that was it, the other girls had already sacrificed; they had burned their hands for the test. *But my hand isn't burned. It couldn't have sunburned with such little exposure to the sun. How can I prove that I am willing to make sacrifices to be with Richard?* What else had Richard said? Violet gasped as she remembered: *I would walk through fire to be with you.*

Violet knew what she had to do. She glanced around the room to make sure that no one was watching her. The other three were all preoccupied with watching the reddening of their skin and were paying her no mind.

Violet walked over to a writing table where one of the few candles that illuminated the room sat. She put her back to the others so that they couldn't see what she was doing. Violet gritted her teeth, then thrust her hand into the flame.

The pain seared through her. Violet wanted to jerk her hand away, but she forced herself to hold it for a moment. She finally pulled it out of the flame and stared down at the angry red of the skin. She collapsed onto a chair and tried not to whimper.

The queen returned with the king, the steward, and Richard. They led the girls out of the dark room and to the great hall. There Celeste, Goldie, and Ruth presented their burned hands in turn. Finally, Violet presented her hand, which had begun to blister.

"What have you done to yourself?" Richard exclaimed when he saw it. Violet gave him a tight smile. "Only what you would do for me."

"I'll have someone come to your room to look at that," the queen said, giving Violet a thoughtful look.

"Thank you, Majesty."

"The four of you shall continue on to the final challenge," the king said.

Violet made it to her room before the tears came. Genevieve exclaimed in despair over her injured hand. "This was stupid; there had to have been something else you could have done," Genevieve said.

Violet shook her head. "I sacrificed. That's what was required."

"Richard wouldn't have wanted you to hurt yourself, though. Why did you leave your hand in the fire for so long?"

"I had to be sure."

An older gentleman arrived and put a poultice on her hand, which quenched some of the heat. Once he had left, Genevieve glared at her.

"You know the goal is to marry the prince, right?" Genevieve said.

Violet was irritated. "Yes, what's your point?"

"You can't marry him if you're dead. Just promise me you won't do something stupid tomorrow."

"I would like to promise that," Violet said. She yawned. "All I can promise at the moment, though, is that I'm going to bed."

As she drifted off to sleep, however, she knew that Genevieve was right to be worried. The tests were becoming harder, and there was no telling what she'd have to do next.

CHAPTER TWELVE

Violet woke to feel Duke licking her good hand. The room was pitch-dark, and Violet sat up slowly, lit the candle by her bed, and took the scroll from him.

My Beloved Violet, I was horrified to see what you had done to yourself on my behalf. Dearest, I am not worth injuring yourself. Please do not do something so foolish again. I will find some way for us to be together, no matter the cost. Yours always, Richard.

She reread the letter twice. No mention of the final test. If anything Richard sounded more doubtful of the outcome than he had in previous letters. She scratched Duke's ears before blowing out the candle and falling back asleep.

The next day Violet was surprised to discover that more people were arriving at the castle. Rows and rows of coaches pulled up outside, and she watched out the window as nobles from several different countries arrived. She could see some of the girls who had chosen to stay despite no longer being in the competition greeting friends and relatives. Even if they hadn't won, it seemed everyone was excited. She thought back to her own feelings of excitement when she had first heard there would be a royal wedding. Apparently, that was one feeling peasant and noble shared alike. How long ago that moment seemed, and now here she was in the castle, doing everything she could to make sure the royal wedding would be her wedding.

"Who are all those people?" Genevieve asked, coming to stand next to her.

"I think they are here to see the final challenge and participate in the Feasting. Several people from Goldie's and Ruth's kingdoms have arrived," Violet said, pointing to two tight little clusters. Ruth was embracing people who looked to be family members. Goldie was greeting her guests more formally, and Violet remembered with a pang that she had lost both her parents. She wondered which of the men standing near her was her villainous uncle, or if he had decided to stay home and plot against her. She shivered.

"Who is that group?" Genevieve asked, pointing to a large cluster of people who stood apart from the rest.

"Celeste's parents—and it looks like every living relative she has is with them," Violet said, overcome with a wave of sadness. She dearly wished she could be greeting her own parents.

"How's your hand?"

"It hurts a lot," she admitted.

The morning passed without a mention of the final test. With the castle bursting with even more people, it seemed that there was nowhere to go to have some solitude. Violet escaped to the garden, where she spent several hours talking with Genevieve and Arianna. They had asked Goldie to join them, but she had looked miserable following the arrival of the nobles from her country and seemed to want to be left alone. When dinnertime came, the great hall was crowded with all the newcomers.

Violet was surprised when the steward bade her sit with Celeste, Goldie, and Ruth at the end of the table closest to Richard and his parents. Violet looked regretfully at her usual seat next to Genevieve. She wasn't excited to be seated next to Celeste.

Violet became anxious as the meal progressed and still nothing was said about the final test. She found herself moving her food around on her plate instead of eating. Just before the meal drew to a close, the king stood, and silence fell on the room.

"Majesties and Highnesses, Lords and Ladies, you all know why we are here. One of these four fair princesses will marry our son and become the new princess of Cambria. They have each passed five challenges and are worthy of the greatest honors that can be bestowed."

The waiting throng applauded, and Violet felt herself blush.

The king continued. "This week we have set forth

many challenges, and these princesses have nobly endeavored to pass them. In order to ensure that each girl was thoroughly tested, the true nature of each test was kept a secret. Until now."

Violet turned and locked eyes with Genevieve, who nodded and smiled.

"In the first test we asked the princesses to choose between silk and cotton threads. All of the threads were silk. However, each girl was then asked to listen to a petition—and to determine which petitioner was lying and which was telling the truth. Those who could tell the difference passed that test. Discernment was the key."

Violet gasped as she remembered being asked about the two farmers disputing water rights. So *that* had been the real test. Genevieve had been right. Not only were all the threads silk; it was not the real test. That was why each of them had chosen differently among the threads and yet been allowed to continue on.

"The girls believed that suffering the pain of a single lost hair was the second test. In truth the second test was how they handled the loss of a single subject—in this case the servant Mary, with whom each of them had interacted only briefly. Those girls who showed concern were allowed to continue on to the next challenge. Compassion was the key."

Violet began to shake. She had not observed Celeste upon hearing the news of Mary's passing, but she was surprised that Celeste had been able to have a thought for anyone other than herself. She must have, though, or she would not have passed that challenge.

"I am happy to announce that there was a bit of deception on our part in that round. Mary is alive and well." King Charles stretched out his hand in the direction of the kitchen, and there stood Mary. She smiled and curtsied. Violet felt joy knowing that the woman was alive.

"For the third test the girls were asked to walk barefoot across the grass, with the only possible results being injury or elimination. While some were injured, one extensively, another refused to bend to the task and another risked exposure as a cheater to pursue what she wanted most."

There were murmurs from the crowd, and Violet felt her cheeks burning. That whole time, and she hadn't been fooling anyone. All that stress, and Richard's parents had known exactly what it was that she was doing with the berries.

The king continued. "We were not actually testing the sensitivity of their feet but the stoutness of their heart. For this test courage was the key. The courage to do what you must, the courage to take a stand, or the courage to risk everything you have for what you want most."

Violet looked at Arianna, who was smiling.

"The fourth test came when most of the princesses became ill from the food they ate. While some thought we were testing to see if their stomachs were too sensitive for peasant food, this test was devised to measure something quite different. We wanted to see how the girls would respond in the face of adversity, whether they could continue on despite hardship. Perseverance was the key."

"I said so!" Violet heard Genevieve exclaim.

"The fifth test, a test of burning the princesses' delicate skin, was in fact a test to see who understood sacrifice. We asked these ladies to sacrifice something of value, their beauty."

Violet smiled while looking at her still bandaged hand. No one could say she hadn't passed that test.

"This leaves us with one final test, a test that we shall conduct here with all of you as witness."

Violet felt her heart sink as she waited to hear the challenge.

"Each princess will tell us why she would be the best person to marry our son."

The king sat down amidst the sudden uproar. Violet stared dumbfounded at Goldie. Violet knew nothing of speaking in front of a large group of people, and she doubted she could convince anyone that she was the most worthy princess.

"Princess Celeste will go first," the queen said.

Celeste rose to her feet, and the crowd quieted. She was calm, composed, and sure of herself. Her eyes swept everyone in the room, and Violet couldn't help but admire her poise. "Long has there been bad blood between Cambria and Lore. These are old feuds whose time has passed. An alliance between Lore and Cambria will ensure peace between these two great kingdoms, and their combined strength will discourage aggression in others. I bring the heart and goodwill of my people. I also bring the wisdom and experience to rule at your son's side."

She took her seat amidst loud applause, particularly from the many Lorians who were present. Violet stared down at her injured hand, trying to decide what she would say.

"Princess Ruth, would you please speak?" the queen asked.

Ruth stood. Her red hair was piled high on her head, standing straighter than she managed to stand. Her hands were shaking, and she kept her eyes fixed on the table. "I have passed every test. I am the most sensitive princess of the four of us. I also know how difficult it can be to lead. Please choose me."

Princess Ruth sat down to a scattering of applause. Violet's heart began to race as she prayed she could do better.

"Princess Violet, why are you the best choice to marry our son?"

Violet rose to her feet, took a deep breath, and looked the queen in the eyes.

"I am the best choice for the simple reason that I love your son more than anything. I have left my home to be here. I have sacrificed much, including my family and my dignity, attempting to pass these tests. I know that I have demonstrated the qualities that you are looking for in the new princess of Cambria. I have no kingdom, no riches, no alliances to bring to this marriage. I can offer nothing but myself, but I believe that to be of great value. And I would cherish every day I had with Richard and live it as though it were my last."

Violet sat back in her chair and heard a few people applauding for her, though she suspected it was her friends.

"And Princess Goldie, what do you have to say?"

Goldie rose to her feet. Her perfect ringlets dusted her shoulders, and looking at her, Violet knew she would be a great queen. "Of everyone here I have the most to offer and the most to gain from an alliance with Cambria. I do not need to tell you the wisdom of that. However, I don't believe that is the question. You haven't asked me what's best for Cambria, but what is best for your son. I know in my heart that Violet is best for your son. She inspires friendship in those who would be rivals. She has compassion for others, the likes of which I have never seen. She understands hardship in a way none of the rest of us ever will, and yet she has the courage of a lion. She has pledged to me her aid, when I made no such pledge to her. She loves your son. She loves Cambria. But even more than that, she *is* Cambria."

Goldie sat down and gave Violet a small smile. Violet just stared at her in return. "You are a true queen," Violet said, reaching out to take Goldie's hand. Finally understanding the qualities that made a queen, she could think of no higher compliment.

"As you will be shortly," Goldie said, squeezing her hand.

Violet glanced toward Richard and saw his parents whisper briefly to each other. Then the king stood up again, and the room fell silent. "All four young women have exceptional qualities. This final test, one of self-confidence, has been most illuminating. The queen and I will spend tonight thinking and discussing what has happened here. In the morning we will make it known who our son will marry—Celeste or Violet."

Pandemonium broke out as roars of excitement went up from the onlookers. There were a few disappointed exclamations that punctuated as well, but they were mostly drowned out by the clamoring of a hundred voices. Violet turned to Goldie. "What just happened?"

Goldie shook her head. "It's just you and Celeste now. Tomorrow we all will know who will marry Prince Richard and become the future queen of Cambria."

Violet looked up at Richard and tried to smile but couldn't. The thought of waiting another minute without knowing her fate was more than she could bear.

"What do I do now?" she asked Goldie.

"Unfortunately, you wait."

Arianna and Genevieve came up to hug her, but Violet felt as one in a dream. At last the steward approached her.

"Their Majesties have requested that you and Princess Celeste be moved to more comfortable rooms for the night while you await their decision."

"But I like my room," Violet said, panicking at the thought of being alone. She knew she wouldn't be able to sleep, and she was counting on Genevieve to keep her from pacing all night long.

"Nevertheless, a special room has been prepared."

Her friends each gave her a quick hug, and then Violet found herself following the steward. She was surprised when he didn't lead her over to the staircase but instead past the throne room. They continued on, and she was surprised to discover another corridor of doors that she hadn't seen before. The steward came to a stop before a great wooden door that was elaborately carved with flowers and gargoyles, and he opened it.

The room was empty except for a bed. Violet came to an abrupt stop and stared at it. There had to be at least twenty mattresses stacked one on top of the other. A ladder was propped up against the foot of the bed to allow the sleeper to climb up.

"I'm supposed to sleep up there?" Violet asked in disbelief.

"Oh, yes, and you should be honored. Not just any guest is invited to sleep in this room. It's a special room, and you will find that the bed is the softest you've ever experienced."

"I don't think I'll be able to sleep tonight," Violet admitted.

"You must at least try. Your things will be brought to you later so you can refresh yourself."

Violet sighed. She wished she could sneak back to her old room with Genevieve and spend the night talking with her, but it probably wouldn't do to insult the generosity of Richard's parents, if they had specially selected this room for her. Resigned, Violet climbed the ladder carefully and finally settled onto the pile of mattresses. It was wonderfully soft, and she realized that she was incredibly tired. Her eyes closed, and Violet fell into a deep sleep.

Richard glared at both his parents, who were sitting serenely in front of the hearth in their chambers, sipping spiced cider as though they were discussing nothing more important than what to have for breakfast.

"You must tell me which one you plan to choose as my bride," Richard insisted.

"Why, so you can run away with Violet if we plan on choosing Celeste?" his father asked.

"So I can properly prepare myself for tomorrow, my wedding, my future."

"Patience is the one virtue we didn't teach him well," his mother remarked to his father.

Richard felt like he was going to lose his mind. His life and happiness hung in the balance, and his parents wanted to lecture him on patience. "Just tell me who!" he pleaded through clenched teeth.

"The truth is, we don't know who it will be yet," his father said with a sigh.

"What do you mean, you don't know? What else could you possibly need to learn about them to make a decision?" Richard asked. Then, suddenly, it came to him. "There's a final test, isn't there?" he asked.

"Yes," his mother said, so quietly he almost didn't hear her.

"Why didn't you tell me?"

"Because we didn't want either Celeste or Violet to know there was one additional test," the king said.

Richard stared at his father's face, wondering if his father knew or only suspected that he had been warning Violet about the challenges. Richard's mother, though, was the one to break the stalemate.

"We know that you've been passing information on to Violet."

"How do you know?" Richard asked.

"You are our son," she said.

"We would have been disappointed if you had left everything to chance," Charles said.

Richard stared at them. They continued to sip their cider, and from the looks on their faces he knew he would get nothing more out of them. Richard excused himself. There was nothing he could do to help Violet through the last test. That left him only one choice. Outside, Richard saddled up Baron, and soon they were racing toward Violet's home.

When Prince Richard arrived at the small farmhouse, it was the middle of the night. He wished he had another choice but to wake the occupants at such a late hour. Time was running out, though.

Richard knocked lightly on the wooden door, and not long afterward a light flared on inside. William opened the door just as raindrops began to fall.

"Your Highness!" William exclaimed.

"I'm terribly sorry to bother you so late. We need to talk," Richard said.

The bad people were coming. She could feel them, hear them. They were running through the castle, shouting and angry. There were torches that blazed so hot. She could hear screaming. Her mother! There was the sound of a sword striking another sword and then a terrible silence. Hands were reaching for her, but she hit at them. She was afraid, and she didn't want to leave. Where would she go? Who would take care of her and love her?

More darkness, more shouting. She was so very frightened, and so was the woman, not her mother, but always so nice. She could smell the fear coming off of her. They ran, faster and faster. But she knew they would never escape. The bad people would always follow, and they would find her. She screamed, but no sound would come out.

Then it was daylight, and she was playing in a field. Her father was coming to her, and he was crying. Her brother was dead. But he wasn't really her brother—how come she knew that but no one else did?

And there, just behind her father's shoulder, ever leering, ever mocking, was the shadow. She tried to run, but the shadow reached out for her with spindly arms and grabbed hold of her. She tried to get away, but it was stronger than she was, and it caught her clothes and hair!

Violet woke up screaming. She sat straight up, panting for breath. She was drenched in sweat, and the pile of mattresses shook slightly from side to side. She lay back down, heart pounding in terror. *You're okay*, Violet told herself repeatedly, until she started to believe it.

Finally, exhaustion took hold, and she fell into a fitful sleep. Then the nightmares started all over again.

Chapter Thirteen

When Violet finally woke in the morning, she was exhausted. Genevieve arrived with her three maids, and together they made a production out of getting Violet dressed for the day.

"You look perfect," Genevieve said, stepping back to admire her handiwork.

"I wish I felt perfect," Violet joked.

Genevieve hugged her. "You're going to be just fine. I know they're going to choose you."

"A dog didn't happen to tell you that, did he?" Violet asked weakly.

"No, but he might as well have. You're the best choice for Richard, for Cambria, in every way."

"Thanks. Now let's just hope that the king and queen agree."

The steward announced, "It's time," before exiting as swiftly as he had entered.

Violet sighed. "I have a bad feeling about this," she admitted.

"It's going to work out; you'll see. Just be yourself," Genevieve said.

As Violet swept out of the room, she was surprised to find Arianna and Goldie waiting for her in the hallway.

"You didn't think we'd miss your moment of triumph, did you?" Arianna asked with a smile.

They all linked arms and walked to the throne room. Once inside, Violet advanced down the length of the room, as her three friends moved to take their places in the gathering crowd of onlookers. Violet stood before the king and queen. She knew that Genevieve and her maids had done their best, but the series of nightmares had taken its toll. Violet just hoped she looked better than she felt. A murmur rippled through the crowd, and she turned to see Celeste enter.

The other girl had never looked more stunning. Violet held back a sigh of frustration. Celeste seemed to float along the floor rather than walk. Her skin was porcelain and radiant. Even Celeste's hand that had suffered the sunburn seemed restored.

Standing next to Violet, Celeste gave her a pitying smile. Violet turned and looked back at Richard and his parents, who were seated on the three thrones. Richard looked tired and haggard, as though he hadn't slept at all. He stared at Violet intently, as if trying to send her a message with his eyes, but she couldn't read his expression.

"Good morning," the queen said, addressing them both.

"Good morning," Celeste and Violet both responded.

"Violet, how did you sleep?"

Violet smiled. "It was the most comfortable bed I have ever slept on. It would have been perfect except I was troubled by nightmares most of the night."

"I'm sorry to hear that," the queen said. She turned to Celeste. "And what about you, dear? How did you sleep?"

"It was dreadful, Your Majesty. I tossed and turned but could find no rest, for something was poking into my back and caused me such pain that I am bruised all over."

"How terrible," the queen said.

"Fortunately, I found this under the bottom mattress," Celeste said, holding up a hard, wrinkled black pea. "Once I removed it, I slept beautifully."

"No nightmares for you, then?" the king asked.

"Not one."

Violet stared in horror at the pea in Celeste's hand. A final test. And she had failed. A final test. And she hadn't even thought to check under the mattresses. Violet should have known the moment she saw the towering stack that there was something wrong.

She hung her head. She had lost. Not only had she lost Richard, but she had also put the daughter of Lore onto the Cambrian throne.

There was a long silence. There was a rustling of cloth, and Violet looked up as the queen descended from her throne and came to stand before Celeste. The queen took the pea from Celeste's hand and held it aloft for all to see. Then, very carefully, she stepped back up onto the dais, where she presented the king with the pea before reclaiming her throne.

The king turned the pea over in his hand before closing his fist around it. "Violet."

"Yes, Your Majesty?"

"Did you find a pea under your mattresses?"

She shook her head in misery. "I felt nothing beneath the mattresses, so I did not think to look."

She glanced at Richard and could tell from his stricken expression that he'd had no advance knowledge of this test.

The king addressed Celeste. "Your cold and suspicious heart has led you to look for something under the mattress and brought you to find this pea. And that is exactly what you shall take away from here. No one is capable of feeling a pea beneath twenty mattresses. Not physically, at any rate."

The king turned to Violet. "This pea, like the pea that was placed under the mattresses in the room you slept in last night, is enchanted. For those with true nobility of spirit, it gives them nightmares. First your character and now your spirit have been tested, and we find you worthy to marry our son."

Violet was sure she had misheard. She turned to look at Richard, and the joy on his face told her that she hadn't. She heard squeals of joy from her friends, who were watching. Before Violet could say anything in response, a man wearing a crown swaggered forward.

"I am Gustav, king of Lore, and you cannot choose this girl over my daughter. She's not even a princess!"

Violet felt white hot anger flash through her toward the king of Lore. He was responsible for the slaughter of the Cambrian royal family, her family.

"Actually, she is a princess," Richard said, rising. "She is the true princess of Cambria." Prince Richard signaled and the crowd parted to reveal a familiar face.

"Father Paul!" Violet exclaimed.

The priest smiled at Violet and then turned to address the others. The crowd that had begun to applaud quieted as people stared from him to Gustav and back.

"The night of the massacre, a nursemaid, whom I knew, rescued the infant princess from the castle. She came to me in confidence for help, and I advised her to place the child in the hands of a loyal farmer and his wife, whom I trusted. I tried to throw any assassins off of the nursemaid's trail as I rendered aid to the injured at the castle. Shortly after seeing the child safe, the woman, Eve, died of an injury she sustained in the flight. She is buried in the churchyard. Violet is the child she carried away from the castle that night. Violet is the true heir of Cambria."

Stunned, Violet watched as Richard's parents stood from their thrones and then bowed to her. Richard did so a moment later. Her heart began to pound as all around her people knelt down. Violet saw Genevieve, Goldie, and Arianna, who all flashed her huge smiles before kneeling too. Violet turned slowly in a circle, looking at all who knelt before her. All except one. She stared for a moment at King Gustav and knew something was wrong.

"Time to finish what was started," the king of Lore roared, drawing his sword.

He leaped at her and grabbed her by the throat. Violet struggled, twisting in his strong arms and scratching at the king's eyes. A dozen Lorian "nobles" shed their cloaks to reveal the clothes of soldiers. They circled Violet, swords brandished. Too late she recognized all of Celeste's guests for what they really were.

With a shout Richard ordered the Cambrian men present to fight. Violet bit Gustav's hand. He roared in pain and then struck her across the temple with the hilt of his sword. Everything went black.

Richard tried to reach Violet, but too many fighters blocked his way. He shouted in rage as he saw Gustav strike his beloved. Her body went limp, and Gustav tossed her over his shoulder before disappearing with Celeste at his side.

A moment later more men wielding swords poured into the great hall. Richard grabbed a sword and began to fight his way through the Lorian soldiers, heading for the spot where he had last seen King Gustav. Nobles from several countries scurried to get away from the fighting, while others drew weapons and joined the fray, trying to fight off the Lorian soldiers.

Richard kept twisting and turning, trying to make his way after Gustav and Violet. He passed Arianna, who was brandishing a weapon of her own and trying to get Genevieve and several others clear of the fighting. Richard finally reached the exit to the hall and saw Gustav disappear into the gardens with Violet still over his shoulder.

Violet woke as she hit the ground. It was raining. Another storm had come, and the king of Lore was trying to finish what he had started during a storm so many years before. She drew in a ragged breath and couldn't believe she was about to die. She opened her eyes and looked up at King Gustav and Celeste. Her head was throbbing, and a thin trickle of blood was dripping into her eye. She blinked fiercely. The father and daughter, arguing about where to go next, didn't notice that Violet was stirring.

Violet glanced around her. She was in the castle garden, not that far from the fountain. She sat up slowly, but neither Gustav nor Celeste paid her any attention. Coiling her muscles, Violet sprang to her feet and began to run.

There were shouts behind her, which spurred her on faster. In front of Violet she saw the outer wall of the hedge maze. She ran along the side of it until she found an opening and then dashed inside. Two quick left turns, followed by a right, and then Violet slowed so that she could get her bearings—and listen for her pursuers.

Violet heard Gustav and Celeste enter the maze, quarreling, and she tried to determine which path they took by listening for their footsteps. Her temple hurt, and she was feeling light-headed, but Violet walked deeper into the maze, and the blackness of the sky caused it to grow as dark as night. The rain further obscured her vision.

Violet pictured the part of the maze she had already traveled. Beneath her feet a twig snapped, and Violet halted for a moment.

"That was her!" Gustav bellowed from somewhere in the leafy maze.

"Yes, but where?" Celeste asked, frustration in her voice.

"How should I know? You're the one who has been at the castle. How come you've never explored the maze?"

"I didn't think it was going to be necessary," Celeste retorted.

Violet began to move again but stepped more gingerly. She shook her head. Back when she was a farmer's daughter, she had thought about entering the maze contest for the Feasting. Now she was a princess. Instead of racing through the maze in an attempt to win a prize, she was slinking through the maze in an attempt to save her life.

Sounds of fighting began to reach her ears, and she realized there must have been more Lorian soldiers present than anyone could have guessed. Again Cambria was at war with Lore. This time, though, Violet swore that no one in the royal family would come to harm.

The storm intensified until she couldn't see at all. Violet paused. She placed a hand on each hedge wall and kicked off her shoes so that she could better feel the ground. Mud oozed between her toes. She continued moving even though she could no longer see anything. When she came to a break in the wall, she took the path.

Violet could hear Gustav as he moved through the maze, but she could no longer hear Celeste. She sensed something move in the path ahead of her. Violet froze and strained ears and eyes. She realized, almost too late, that Gustav and Celeste had split up.

Violet held her breath and moved forward on silent feet. When she was close enough to touch Celeste, she tapped her on the shoulder. The other girl twisted with an exclamation, and Violet hit her as hard as she could.

Celeste crumpled silently to the ground, and Violet stepped over her and kept moving. She would send someone to fetch her when the situation was under control. Violet could hear the fighting just outside the maze walls and prayed that Richard was safe.

Then she heard Gustav shout. It sounded like he might have tripped over Celeste. This gave Violet an idea. She felt for and found a slight hollow at the bottom of one of the hedge walls. She lay down and pushed her body flush with the wall. And then she waited.

Violet stayed still for what felt like an eternity. But she heard Gustav's footsteps before she could see him. She held her breath as he approached and then walked by her. It was then that Violet reached out and grabbed King Gustav's ankle, yanking it backward as hard as she could, with a twist.

There was a snap as he fell with a scream. Violet leaped to her feet and snatched King Gustav's sword from his hand. She swung it with the thought of killing him. At the last moment she twisted her wrist and knocked him unconscious, as he had done to her. She turned and ran back to the entrance of the maze, retracing her steps.

Richard met her there, sword drawn and breathing ragged.

"Are you okay?" they asked each other simultaneously.

"Yes," she said, kissing him.

When they broke apart, Violet told Richard where she had left Gustav and Celeste in the maze and that they needed attention.

"The fighting's almost over. Most of the Lorian soldiers have been captured," he said, sheathing his own sword and taking the one she still held.

Several Cambrians ran to assist Violet and Prince Richard, and Richard directed them into the maze to fetch the Lorian king and his daughter. Then Richard and Violet made their way back to the castle.

In the great hall Violet was reunited with Goldie,

Genevieve, and Arianna, none the worse for wear. She looked for Father Paul, desperately wanting to talk to him, to ask him about her mother, but she didn't see him.

Everyone slowly regrouped in the throne room as servants and soldiers worked to clear the wounded. Celeste and her father were being treated elsewhere for their injuries, Violet learned, though their future was still uncertain. It seemed that several of the other nobles had opposed Gustav's plan, wanting to continue the peace with Cambria.

Once again seated on her throne, Queen Martha looked unruffled, as though they had only been discussing the weather instead of fighting for their lives. King Charles, like his son, was slightly disheveled from the fighting. With a start Violet saw that Father Paul was with them.

"Now, where were we?" the king inquired.

Father Paul cleared his throat. "Last night the prince went to the home of Violet's adopted parents. I was staying the night after having given her mother a new herbal potion to try and ease her pain."

"How is she?" Violet interrupted, not caring if it was princesslike or not, just needing to know.

Father Paul smiled at her. "When I left, she seemed to be doing better. I think there's cause to hope even that she might recover."

Violet felt her knees buckle, and she sagged against Arianna in relief.

Father Paul resumed his story. "Prince Richard

shared everything that had transpired here during the competition, and he asked whether or not it could be proved that Violet was the true princess of Cambria. Given everything that has transpired, I knew the time had finally arrived to reveal my part in the child's disappearance. I have known the truth and have kept it secret for seventeen years. Violet is the princess."

"It's so hard to believe," Violet whispered.

"It is you," Father Paul assured her. "I came back with Richard so that I could tell what I knew."

"And we thank you," the queen said.

"Thank you, Father Paul," Violet said, voice trembling.

"I never intended to keep your whereabouts a secret forever, my dear; just until I knew that it was safe," he said with a smile. "Prince Richard convinced me that it was."

"Not as safe as I thought," Richard grimaced.

"And my mother might recover?"

"It looks very good. Of course, it would help if she had constant care and good food. That's why Prince Richard has arranged for your parents to arrive here tomorrow morning to help you celebrate."

"Celebrate?" Violet asked.

"Our wedding," Richard said, moving next to Violet and taking her hand in his. The look that he gave her sent shivers through her, and she began to smile.

☙ ☙ ☙

After dinner Violet and Richard found a stolen moment alone. He led her upstairs, navigating swiftly through the maze of hallways, but wouldn't tell her where they were going.

"Does this have something to do with that surprise you promised me?" she asked.

He smiled. "Yes, it does."

A minute later they were standing inside one of the private chambers. "These are my rooms, soon to be ours," Richard said.

Violet felt herself blush.

"I wanted to show you this," he said, indicating a large tapestry on the wall near his writing desk.

She studied it and after only a moment realized it depicted the assassination of her parents. Richard stood quietly beside her as she looked at it.

"I looked at this tapestry every day as a child," he murmured. "And yet I was blind to the most significant detail until just recently."

"What is that?" Violet asked.

He pointed toward the far side. "There, the woman holding the baby, leaving the room."

"Yes?"

"The child has a crown on her head. And she is very much alive as opposed to her parents. Violet, that's you."

Violet raised her hand to touch the weaving. *Me, that was me, smuggled out of the castle right under the noses of the murderers.* She felt tears sting her eyes as she said a silent thank-you to the nurse, Eve. Had the weaver known or guessed that Violet had survived that night?

To Richard she said, "Thank you."

The whole kingdom was poised to celebrate the High Feast like never before. The return of the princess and the new victory over Lore had spurred the people on to increased zeal, and the festivities of the first two days of the Feasting had been larger and noisier than anyone could ever remember. Violet had even managed to get her new friends into the kitchen to try their hands at pie baking for the contest. The cooks had looked on in dismay as Genevieve, Goldie, and Arianna got more flour on themselves than in the pies.

When High Feast Day, the third day of the festival, arrived, Violet was breathless with excitement and anticipation. "How do I look?" Violet asked, smoothing down her dress. The gown was white with ribbons of green and gold—the national colors of Cambria—streaming from the bodice and flowing toward the floor. Matching ribbons of green and gold had been braided into her hair, which Genevieve and all three of her maids had spent an hour on. The skirts of Violet's dress were so full that she had trouble moving about her room without knocking things over. She had asked to be allowed to spend the last few days in her room with Genevieve prior to the wedding, and her friend had already picked up half a dozen things that Violet's skirts had knocked over that morning.

"Beautiful," Genevieve said.

"Like a princess," Arianna confirmed.

"Like the most beautiful bride Cambria has ever seen," Goldie said.

Violet hugged her friends. In less than an hour she and Richard would be married. It still took her breath away to think about it.

There was a knock on the door, and Goldie went to get it. "You have visitors, Violet."

Violet turned to see two elegantly dressed women walk into the room arm in arm. The first was Richard's mother, and the second was hers. Violet felt tears of joy stinging her eyes. Sarah's cough was getting better each day, and although she was very weak, she had begun to get out of bed. Still, Queen Martha had spent hours with Sarah, and the two had enjoyed planning every moment of the wedding together. Violet marveled as she saw the queen holding up her adopted mother and was touched by how generous Richard's mom was and how caring.

Violet's parents had been invited to live in the castle, but they weren't entirely sure they were ready to give up farming. Violet had persuaded them to stay for a couple of weeks after she married Richard. It would give her mom more time to recover, and when Thomas had shown up the day before for the festivities, he had very solemnly promised to run the farm in their absence.

Violet embraced the two women and then offered

them seats. "Violet, have you seen the portrait of your mother?" Sarah asked.

Violet nodded. The portraits of the former royal family had been in storage for nearly seventeen years. King Charles had had the large canvases brought out, and Violet had been delighted to see that there was a family resemblance.

"The same beautiful violet eyes. That night you arrived here, I felt you had to be related," Queen Mary said, with a smile.

"I'm still surprised you let me in the door, as wretched as I looked that night," Violet said.

"But if I remember correctly, you looked gorgeous by dinner. I knew that dress would look perfect on you."

"So, it was you who sent the clothes?" Violet asked.

"Yes. I always believed that you had survived, and I had hoped someday we would find you. When it looked like you might actually be the princess, how could I not make sure you were at least attired like one?"

Violet smiled. "I have so much to thank you both for."

"I did bring you something for good luck today. You can put it in your shoe or your bodice," the queen said.

"What is it?"

"Hold out your hand."

Violet did as instructed, and into it the queen dropped a single black pea. Violet stared at its round black shape before looking up at the other woman.

"It's from underneath your mattresses. That pea helped bring you to this day. And now I think you've had quite enough of nightmares, so never fall asleep near it again."

Violet started laughing.

Out in the hall she heard a familiar voice and smiled. "What's so funny in there?" she heard her father ask.

"Nothing!" Violet called back.

"May we come in?" Richard asked, trying to sound innocent.

"No," Violet said, walking close to the door. She touched it and could feel his presence on the other side.

"This door can't keep us apart forever," he joked.

Violet smiled and looked at the pea. "Nothing can keep us apart ever again."

"You know, in less than an hour everything changes," he whispered.

"I know," Violet whispered back, glancing out the window at the gathering storm clouds and smiling.

DON'T MISS THIS MAGICAL TITLE
IN THE ONCE UPON A TIME SERIES!

Midnight Pearls

DEBBIE VIGUIÉ

It should have been the happiest day of her life, but instead it was a living nightmare. Pearl slowly fingered the fabric of her pale blue gown and closed her eyes. Fat tears squeezed out from beneath her eyelids and rolled down her cheeks.

The bell of the chapel began to ring. It was ringing for her. Its keening was her death sentence, its steady beat her death march. She felt herself begin to shake. Today was the last day of her freedom, her last taste of joy. She opened her eyes and stared down at her slippers. They gleamed softly white, mocking her. Today was supposed to be the happiest day of her life, for today she would become a bride.

She looked back upon her life and saw how every step had led her here. Where had it all gone wrong? What could she have changed?

She closed her eyes again and prayed for death.

The fisherman sat quietly in his boat staring at the darkening skies. The sun should have stood directly overhead, marking midday, but instead it was obscured by angry clouds that seemed to grow thicker by the moment. He squinted, staring at the horizon. The leathery skin of his face crinkled around his hazel eyes. A storm was coming up fast, too fast. A stiff wind suddenly sprang to life, roaring across the bow of the boat and bringing with it the unmistakable smell of rain. It was time to head for shore.

The fish had been acting strange all day, nervous, as though there was a predator lurking in the darkening water. He had been out since noon, and not a single one had found its way into his nets. Still, he had seen the dancing shadows and quick flashes of silver that indicated their presence. He quickly pulled the woven rope nets in and secured them.

A raindrop splatted on his nose and a shiver danced up his spine. *Finneas*, he thought, *you'd better get yourself home fast.*

No sooner had he picked up the oars and began to row than the heavens let loose. The ocean began to heave, and it was all he could do to keep the tiny boat from capsizing.

He strained at the oars with all his might. He had never seen a storm come up so quickly. He should have had time to make it home before the weather became this bad. His arms began to ache with the strain of fighting the waves. A huge one bore down on him, and he saw it through the rain, but it was too late to turn the boat. It crested over the bow and filled the tiny vessel with water.

He had always been careful, always respected the sea not only for what it could give but also for what it could take. He had lost his father and his two brothers to its wrath. His was a family of fishermen eking out a living from the sea. But the sea was a fickle mistress. He remembered the storm that had taken the lives of the other men in his family. Still, he, too, had gone to the sea for his livelihood. It was all he knew.

As wave after wave continued to crash down upon him, he knew that his time had come at last. The sea would claim him this day, and he would never see his beloved Mary again. He whispered a desperate prayer to St. Michael, patron saint of the sea, and another one to King Neptune for good measure. Father Gregory would not be happy about that, but the good father wasn't there to take offense.

A short distance ahead of him he saw a light shimmering in the water that grew brighter as he watched. Was it the angel of death coming to take him? He briefly thought about trying to go around the spot. He was too tired, though, to waste his strength rowing the extra distance. *And if it is the angel of death,* he reasoned, *he'll find me whether I turn the boat or not.* He kept his course, and moments later he was right above the light. He stared down into the water but could see nothing.

Cast out your nets, a voice whispered in his head. Without thinking, Finneas scurried to comply, heaving the nets over the side and dropping them down into the light. Something heavy caught in them, and he feared that between the weight and the raging of the ocean the ropes would snap. He began to pull them in. They held, and the light grew brighter as he kept pulling. At last something broke the surface of the water.

Finneas gasped as the small face of a child looked up at him. She had enormous eyes that shone dark against her pale skin. Her white hair floated on the water, each long strand glimmering with a greenish light—the glow that he had seen. She was caught in his net, and he heaved her into the boat. She sat very still, the blinking of her eyes the only sign of life.

He quickly untangled her until she sat naked and shivering in the bottom of the tiny vessel. He peeled off his coat and wrapped it around her. For a moment he forgot the wind and waves and storm as he stared at her. *What had Father Gregory read from the Good Book that morning? "I will make you fishers of men."*

He smiled reassuringly at the child as he picked up his oars. "We are going to make it, you and I." She just blinked her enormous eyes.

God, Neptune, St. Michael—someone had sent the child to him. He couldn't let her die in the storm. That conviction gave him the will to keep pulling at the oars. At last after what seemed like an eternity, the wind swept aside a curtain of rain and he caught a glimpse of the shore. His heart lifted at the sight, and he pulled on the oars with renewed strength.

Finally they hit the beach. He scrambled out of the boat and began to try to pull it backward onto the sand. Finneas fell to his knees, a sob escaping him. He was too weak. He felt his fingers beginning to slip from the bow when, suddenly, strong hands closed over his and lent their strength. Together they pulled the ship backward up onto the beach.

Finneas collapsed onto the sand gasping and looked up to see his wife. His heart filled at the sight of her face, beautiful in his eyes. "Mary, I thought I'd never see you again."

"And I you," she answered.

He gestured to the boat. "I brought you something."

She looked in and gasped softly. "Oh my."

They made it to the house and barred the door against the lashing rain. Finneas peeled off his wet clothes, depositing them in a heap by the fire and changing into dry ones while Mary wrapped the child in a warm blanket. She sat down with her by the fire and lifted a lock of her wet hair. Finneas noticed that the glow from the child's hair was slowly fading.

He shivered and muttered a silent prayer. Still, as he looked into the little girl's enormous eyes, he couldn't see any evil lurking in them. *If she isn't of the devil, then she has to be from God.* He nodded slowly. She was God's gift to his Mary, who had no child of her own. He placed a hand on Mary's shoulder.

When Mary looked up at him he had no answers for the questions in her eyes. They stared at each other for several minutes before she broke the silence.

"I thought you might be dead," she croaked, her voice hoarse.

"I nearly was," he admitted as he took a seat beside her. "Then I found her—out there in the water. I knew then that I was going to live and that the Good Lord wanted me to bring her home—to you."

Mary gently stroked the girl's hair. "She can't be more than four years old. What do you think she was doing out there by herself?"

Finneas shook his head. "I don't know."

The girl stirred in Mary's arms and stretched her small hand out toward the fire. Her skin was pale, deathly pale. Finneas felt his heart begin to pound. For a moment, when her hand was up in front of the fire, he imagined that he'd been able to see right through the skin, through her very hand, to see the fire glowing on the other side.

He shook his head to clear it. *I'm exhausted, and a*

trick of the light sent my imagination on a flight of fancy. That is all. But beside him he heard Mary gasp, and when she turned to him with fearful eyes he knew that it was no trick and that she had seen it too.

"Wh-what is she?"

He met Mary's eyes. "I don't know and I don't think we want to know."

She nodded slowly, and a silent agreement stretched between them. The child looked up at them questioningly. She stretched out her other hand from beneath the blanket. It was balled into a tight fist. Something dark shone through the cracks between her fingers.

"What have you got, little one?" Finneas asked, reaching gently to take her hand. He pushed at her fingers, and reluctantly her fist began to open.

There in her palm was the largest pearl he had ever seen. It was a shiny, midnight blue color and was almost perfectly round. He had never seen anything like it.

Her small fingers balled around it, and her hand disappeared back beneath the blanket. He laid a hand upon her head. "I think we'll call her Pearl."

Two days later the storm had passed, but the destruction it had left in its wake was staggering. Villages up and down the coast had been destroyed, some of them completely. Worse, several hundred people had been killed.

As Finneas sat beside Mary in church that

Sunday, he fervently thanked God for the safety they had enjoyed. Only a couple of people from their village had lost their lives. The priest solemnly prayed for their souls. In front of Finneas the town blacksmith, Thomas, bowed his head in sorrow. His wife had been one of those who was lost.

Finneas felt guilty for his and Mary's happiness in the face of so much sorrow. Happy they were, though, for little Pearl sat between them. The storm that had brought her to them had made it easy to explain her sudden presence. They had simply told everyone that she was the child of a distant cousin in another village who had been killed in the storm.

That had satisfied the others, although it hadn't stopped them from casting puzzled looks at Pearl. Finneas closed a hand around Pearl's protectively. Maybe with time the sun would tan her unnaturally pale skin, and as she continued to grow, surely she would grow into her long legs.

She looked up at him with her wide, dark eyes and asked him a question. At least, he thought it was a question. He had no way to answer her, though. Whatever language it was she spoke was foreign to him. He thought it might be Italian, but he wasn't sure.

He just shook his head and squeezed her hand. They were working on teaching her English. He just prayed they would be able to communicate quickly before it became too much of a problem.

Mary turned to look at him and he smiled to hide

his concern. He couldn't help but be afraid. Pearl was different; he wasn't sure how or why, but he did know the people of his village. They didn't tolerate anyone or anything that was different. Only five years earlier an angry mob had seized a woman, a traveling gypsy, accused her of Witchcraft, and burned her at the stake. He shuddered at the memory. *And there was nothing I could do to stop it.*

He gripped Pearl's hand even tighter until she began to wriggle her fingers. He had had a nightmare about the villagers trying to do the same to Pearl and him not being able to reach her. He had awoken screaming and soaked in sweat. He had lied to Mary for the first time in his life, telling her he didn't remember the dream. He had vowed, lying there, shivering and praying, that he would do everything in his power to keep them from hurting Pearl. He just continued to smile at Mary, who had enough to worry about without hearing his fears.

When the services were over, he picked Pearl up in his arms. She hadn't yet seemed to master walking. She was trying, but she just went skittering on her long limbs, wobbling back and forth and landing in a heap time after time. *She just needs to grow into her legs,* he thought.

She wrapped her tiny arms around his neck and looked up at him. She asked him what sounded like a question. Her tiny voice lilted as though she was singing. He just shook his head and kissed her cheek.

She held her pearl out to him and he kissed it as

well. Mary had secured it with a thin piece of rope and a loop so that Pearl could wear the shiny orb around her neck. She laughed up at him. Her laughter, at least, he could understand.

That night Finneas sat bolt upright in bed, awakened by a keening sound that split the stillness and reverberated in the air. Chills danced up and down his spine, and fear touched his heart. Beside him Mary sprang from the bed, grabbing for her shawl. They glanced to the bed where Pearl should have been, but it was empty. A hard knot settled in the bottom of his stomach.

They exchanged frightened glances and began to search the cabin. They found her moments later sitting in the kitchen. She was surrounded by dead fish that were scattered about on the kitchen floor. She must have pulled them off the counter and unwrapped them from their protective coverings.

The stench of death was strong, and an unnatural sound was coming from Pearl. She stared up at them and pointed to a dead fish and then to Finneas. His heart began to pound as he realized that she was blaming him for its death.

Mary knelt down and folded the girl in her arms. "Those are fish. We eat the fish so that we can be strong," she tried to explain.

Pearl began to cry and Mary just held her, clearly not knowing what to say. Finally she looked up at Finneas, and he saw the tears shimmering on her cheeks as well. "Clean up the fish and hide them," she instructed him. "We'll keep them out of her sight, at least for now."

Nodding, Finneas did as he was told. The sound of her cries echoed inside his head continuing long after she had fallen asleep in Mary's arms. It had been a completely unnatural sound, unlike anything he had ever heard.

About the Author

DEBBIE VIGUIÉ holds a degree in creative writing from UC Davis. Her Simon Pulse books include the *New York Times* bestselling Wicked series with Nancy Holder, and the novels *Midnight Pearls* and *Scarlet Moon*. She currently lives in Hawaii with her husband, Scott. Visit her at debbieviguie.com.

Love is in the air....

♥ ♥ the romantic comedies ♥ ♥

♥ How NOT to Spend Your Senior Year ♥ Royally Jacked ♥
Ripped at the Seams ♥ Spin Control ♥ Cupidity
♥ South Beach Sizzle ♥ She's Got the Beat ♥
30 Guys in 30 Days ♥ Animal Attraction ♥ A Novel Idea
♥ Scary Beautiful ♥ Getting to Third Date ♥ Dancing Queen ♥
Major Crush ♥ Do-Over ♥ Love Undercover ♥ Prom Crashers
♥ Gettin' Lucky ♥ The Boys Next Door ♥ In the Stars ♥
Crush du Jour ♥ The Secret Life of a Teenage Siren
♥ Love, Hollywood Style ♥ Something Borrowed ♥
Party Games ♥ Puppy Love ♥ The Twelve Dates of Christmas
♥ Sea of Love ♥ Miss Match ♥ Love on Cue ♥ Drive Me Crazy ♥
Love Off-Limits ♥ The Ex Games ♥ Perfect Shot
♥ Hard to Get ♥ At First Sight ♥

From Simon Pulse
PUBLISHED BY SIMON & SCHUSTER

Make a date with Felicity

and look for:

From Simon Pulse ♥ Published by Simon & Schuster

sïmonTeen

Simon & Schuster's **Simon Teen**

e-newsletter delivers current updates

on the hottest titles, exciting

sweepstakes, and exclusive content

from your favorite authors.

Visit **TEEN.SimonandSchuster.com**

to sign up, post your thoughts, and find

out what every avid reader is talking about!

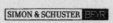